Sharp Edges

By K.L. Middleton

Copyright © 2012 by K.L. Middleton

This book is purely fiction and any resemblances to names, characters, and places are coincidental. The reproduction of this work is forbidden without written consent from the author. The author acknowledges the trademark owners of various products referenced in this work of fiction, which has been used without permission. The publication/use of these trademarks is not authorized, associated with, or sponsored by the trademark owners.

All rights reserved. Without limiting the rights under copyright reserved above, no part of this publication may be reproduced, stored in any form or by any means (electronic, mechanical, photocopying, recording, or otherwise) without the prior written permission of this copyright owner and the above publisher of this book.

Copyedited by: Carolyn M. Pinard
www.thesupernaturalbookeditor.com

To my family,
My friends,
And my readers,
Thank you for supporting me.

Prologue

"I'm hungry," whispered the small voice huddled next to him in the darkness.

"Shh..." he murmured to his three-year-old brother. "She'll hear you."

Tears streamed down the boy's cheeks and his lips began to tremble. "But..."

He clamped a hand over his mouth. "You have to be quiet," he pleaded. "Or... she'll get really mad. You don't want that, do you?"

The boy's large brown eyes widened and he shook his head.

He released his grip. "Okay, then. Don't worry, he'll leave soon and mommy will let us out. Just play with your Legos for now."

His brother wiped his face with the back of his hand and then resumed playing with the small plastic pieces.

"Here," he whispered, turning on the flashlight. He pointed it towards the colorful spaceship. "Better?"

The boy smiled. "Yes."

He sighed and drew his knees up to his chest, wishing his mom would finish with the man in the bedroom so they could come out. They'd been hiding inside for almost an hour, which was much too long for any three-year-old to sit still.

"Keep your brother quiet," she'd warned him, earlier, as she'd applied the black stuff to her eyelashes. "My clients won't come back if they find out I have kids."

His mother was some kind of a massage therapist, and because they lived in a one-bedroom apartment, she made them hide in her walk-in closet whenever the neighbor from across the hall was unavailable to babysit. Tonight was one of those nights.

"Is it almost over?" whispered his brother.

"I don't know," he answered. Once in a while he could hear the man grunt or the bed shake. The noise made him feel funny inside.

"Um...I have to pee."

He sighed. "Too bad, you *have* to hold it."

"But, I need to go really... really... bad."

He gripped his brother's pale, skinny arm and leaned closer. "Hold it," he warned.

The boy put his other hand over his crotch. "But..."

A loud crash from the bedroom startled them both and they could hear their mother whimpering in fear. "Please," she begged. "No more."

Hearing the terror in her voice, he stood up and pushed the door open, ready to do battle for her.

"No!" she hollered in protest, seeing her nine-year-old son step out of the closet.

He froze and stared in shock at the scene before him. Standing above his mother was a sweaty fat man wearing nothing but dark pants, while she was crouched down on her hands and knees on the mattress, naked with angry red marks on her skin.

He clenched his fists. "Leave her alone!" he yelled.

The man pointed a shiny black belt at him and turned toward his mother. "Now who the fuck is that, Karen?"

"Mommy?" cried his little brother, now peeking out from the closet.

His mother groaned. "Shit. Take him and go to the kitchen," she ordered, grabbing her robe from the floor.

"These your brats?" asked the man, a weird smile spreading across his ruddy face.

"Yeah," she mumbled, grabbing her smokes from the nightstand.

"You never mentioned kids."

"Sorry, George," she said, lighting a cigarette. She took a long drag, blew out a cloud of smoke, and pointed towards the door. "Didn't you hear me? Take your brother into the fucking kitchen now!"

"Let's go," he sighed, leading the little boy out of the bedroom.

"But, I still have to go potty," he pouted.

"Mom said we have to go to the kitchen and she's already pissed. Just hold it a little while longer."

His brother brushed a lock of dark hair away from his face and nodded. "Okay."

They stepped into the kitchen and sat down next to each other at the chipped porcelain table. Bored and frustrated, he stared at his clasped hands then shifted his weight back and forth on the wobbly chair, listening to the familiar creaking sound. He knew it was a matter of time before the chair finally collapsed, just like everything else they owned.

"I'm still hungry," whispered his brother, staring longingly at the refrigerator. They hadn't eaten since breakfast and it was now almost bedtime.

"We have to wait until *she* feeds us," he replied, trying to ignore his own hunger pangs.

The boy scowled. "But my tummy's rumbling."

"I know; mine too," he answered, bitterly.

They sat in silence, each lost in their own thoughts. As he mulled over the weird scene back in the bedroom, his eyes drifted to the drained bottle of *Wild Turkey,* sitting on the counter. She loved the brown liquid but it sometimes made her mean. He was relieved to see that the bottle was empty.

Sighing, he sat back in the chair and folded his arms across his chest, wondering what was happening with his mother and the man; it was obvious that she wasn't giving *him* a massage. As he reflected upon this, George stepped into the kitchen and opened up the refrigerator.

"Jesus Christ," he grunted, staring into the empty box. "Nothing but bologna and beer?" he said, scratching his fat, hairy belly. "Fuck it."

The boy watched in anger as the man grabbed what was left of their food, as well as two bottles of his mother's beer, and then closed the refrigerator.

"That's ours," he told George, motioning towards the bologna. "You can't eat that."

The man raised his bushy eyebrows. "Oh, is that so?"

"Yeah," he answered, raising his chin defiantly.

George calmly put the bologna and beer down on the counter, then reached around and grabbed him by the shirt, lifting him out of the chair. "Listen here, tough guy," he growled, "I'm going to teach you a lesson about respecting your elders. Got that?"

"No!" he yelled, pushing at George's sweaty chest, trying to escape.

"What's going on?" interrupted their mother as she stepped into the kitchen, wearing her tattered blue robe.

The man tightened his grip on the boy's shirt. "Me and your boy here are going to have a man-to-man talk," he said. "He needs to learn to respect me, especially now that I'm going to be moving in."

He stared at the man's bloodshot eyes in horror. *Moving in?*

His mother's face paled and she grabbed George's arm. "No. Please. I'll make sure he doesn't backtalk you again."

George backhanded her and she toppled to the ground. "Shut the fuck up, bitch. You still owe me, big time – so guess what? I'm collecting."

Her nose began to bleed and his little brother, whose jeans were wet with urine, rushed to her side, sobbing. She put a protective arm around him and glared at George.

"Don't even think about interfering, again," warned George. "Or I'll make *both* of these little shits pay."

Terrified of the strange gleam in the man's beady eyes, he struggled as hard as he could to get free. "Let me go!" he choked. "Please, let me go!"

George smiled, coldly. "That's it, keep fighting, kid. I like a fighter."

"Please, not my son!" his mother sobbed from the floor. "Do it to me instead. Please!"

George ignored her and dragged him out of the kitchen towards the bedroom, where he spent the next hour, paying off some of his mother's debt.

Chapter One

Twenty-Five Years Later

"Would you look at that?" murmured my best friend, Darcy, squinting across the dark street at the lone figure stretching his hard, sexy calves.

I took a sip of my coffee and chuckled. "Mm hmm…I know."

It was early morning, the sun was just beginning to rise, and we'd been standing outside on my porch, talking about her court appearance scheduled for later in the day. She was going through a nasty divorce, and her ex, Frank, was being a total asshole about settling. Apparently, he'd forgotten about his infidelity and was trying to gain full custody of their five-year-old son, Max, who I'd volunteered to watch while they hashed it out in court.

"Married men shouldn't be allowed to look that freakin' hot," stated Darcy.

"Actually, I don't think he's married," I said, brushing the hair out of my eyes.

We watched in silence as my new neighbor finished his morning routine of stretching his sinewy body parts before taking off for the usual morning run. Today it was already humid, so he was dressed in black shorts and a bright yellow tank top that emphasized his lean, muscular arms. Catching us gawking, he waved and we reciprocated.

Darcy sighed. "You've got it made, Lindsey," she said as we both turned to watch him jog towards the golden-pink sky, admiring his tight buns as they moved beneath the shorts. "You've got a doting husband, a hunky neighbor, and kids who can make themselves breakfast in the morning. Honestly, you make me want to slit my fucking throat."

I choked on my coffee and began laughing. "Darcy! Jeez, don't be so hard on yourself. You're just in a tough place right now. Once this divorce thing is over, you can get on with your life. Besides," I said, "you know very well that I'm always here for you."

She opened up her purse and took out a tube of lipstick. "And I appreciate that, Linds," she said, after applying it generously to her lips. "Really, I do. But what I need is to just get through this nightmare with Frank. Then, I'm going to drop Max off at grandma's for the weekend, find me someone sexy and stimulating who doesn't run on batteries, and top it all off with a bottle of expensive champagne to help me forget about everything else for a few hours."

I raised my eyebrows. "Batteries?"

"I've got to do something," she said dryly. "My vibrator started smoking last night, and not in a good way."

I giggled. "You and that damn thing. I heard you can really hurt something down there if you use it too much."

She waved her hand. "I've used it a thousand times this past year and let me tell you, the hurt is *good*."

Leave it to Darcy.

We'd known each other since grade school, and were been best friends all the way through senior high. Then, she'd taken off for college to become a C.P.A. and I'd stayed behind because I'd gotten pregnant. Fortunately, Scott and I had been madly in love at the time and everything had worked out just fine in the end. We'd gotten married, had two beautiful children, and were now entering our fifteenth year of marriage. Of course, we'd had our occasional fights and disagreements throughout the years, but had always managed to work out the kinks. Life was good and I felt fairly content in it.

"I suppose I should get going," she said, looking at her watch. "I'll be back to pick up Max sometime after two o'clock, if everything goes as planned."

"Okay," I answered, finishing the last of my coffee.

"He'll probably fall asleep soon. Frank had him last night, and didn't drop him off until late."

I nodded. "That's fine. Well, good luck, Darcy. Call me when you can and let me know how it's going."

She nodded and gave me a hug. "Thanks for everything, hon."

"You know I'd do anything for you," I said. "Now, remember – stay strong!"

"I'll try," she said, stepping off the porch. "If I don't get my way, however, I'm going to rip his dick off and stuff it down his skanky girlfriend's throat."

I chuckled and watched as she walked to her Mercedes in her designer suit, expensive haircut, and perfectly-manicured nails. For as long as I could remember, she'd always looked perfect: no blonde hair out of place, flawless makeup, and rail-thin except for the silicone breasts she'd recently purchased after Frank had gone and cheated on her. Those were still fairly new and even I was having a hard time getting used to them. I thought she'd gotten them a little too big, but she wanted to rub them in Frank's face. Well, not literally; he'd lost that privilege.

As I opened the front door, I looked down at my own short, messy nails and sighed. There was a time when *I'd* turn heads, just like Darcy, but these days, I turned nothing but supermarket isles and grilled-cheese sandwiches. I was also about fifteen pounds overweight, give or take five, and the last time I had *my* hair professionally done was six years ago, just before my sister's wedding. She'd made the appointment, paid for it, and dropped me off before I could protest.

"It's my wedding and I want everything perfect," she'd told me. "Including my only sister, so don't argue."

Even I had to admit that I'd looked pretty amazing walking out of the salon that day. My auburn hair had been trimmed, foiled, and styled – and not by my own hands for once. Of course, it had also been outrageously expensive and was something I hadn't repeated on my own. These days, "practical" was my middle name. That meant trimming my own hair, wearing cheap, comfortable clothing, and biting my nails evenly to make sure they all matched. If I did use nail polish, it was the quick-dry stuff that chipped by the end of the day, so I mostly never bothered with that, either. Except for my toenails; for some reason, not having neatly trimmed and polished toenails wasn't even an option for me. Secretly, besides my dark brown eyes, I thought my feet were my best feature, which, come to think of it, *was* a little pathetic.

As I mulled over these things, I stepped into the kitchen where Scott was finishing his morning cup of coffee.

"Good morning," I said.

He glanced at me and smiled. "Good morning. I see that Max is sacked out on the sofa. Today must be the court thing?"

I sighed. "Yeah, it's the big day. Darcy is on pins and needles."

He walked over and kissed my cheek. "I'm sure everything will work out just fine."

"I hope so," I said, leaning into him. "She's been through so much."

He nodded. "Oh, by the way, I have to work late again. This deal is turning out to be a nightmare. The firm we're trying to sign up with isn't happy with anything we've designed. Now we have to start over, all the way from scratch."

Sighing, I moved over to my Keurig and started brewing another cup of coffee. "Damn, I know how hard you've been working on those proposals, too. Well, will you be home in time for dinner?"

He ran a hand threw his wavy, blonde hair and shrugged. "I don't know yet. Listen, just don't even worry about dinner, babe, I'll pick up something on the way home if it gets too late."

"Okay."

"I love you," he said, reaching over and grabbing me around the waist.

"I love you, too. Don't forget about tomorrow night."

He smiled. "Our anniversary? Now, how in the world could I forget about that?"

"Honestly, I wish your parents wouldn't have splurged like they did. Didn't you say they've rented out one of the banquet rooms at the Hyatt?"

He pulled a tendril of my hair playfully. "Yes, they have. But, you know how they live for these things and love doing it for us. They're retired and bored."

And so rich they don't know what to do with all of their money.

"I guess. It's just... I wanted something romantic, you know? Just the two of us," I pouted.

"We'll have all night for that," he said, sliding his hands over my hips.

With his hands gripping my rear and the scent of his cologne teasing my senses, I didn't even care anymore. As long as we'd be celebrating in our own special way after the party, I could live with whatever made him happy. "We do, and I'm looking forward to it."

"Me, too. Well, I'd better go. I'll call you later," he said, releasing me and grabbing his briefcase. "Give the kids a hug for me."

"I will," I said, pushing my bangs out of my eyes once again. I desperately needed a trim and made a mental note to look for the scissors.

I watched him as he left, admiring how polished he looked in his grey Ralph Lauren suit.

After all these years, he was still an incredibly handsome man. It was hard to imagine that we'd been together for over fifteen years, although, I felt like I'd loved him my entire life.

"Morning," mumbled my oldest daughter, Regan, as she shuffled into the kitchen. She'd just turned fourteen and was still at the age where she loved school. She was on the girl's track team, played tennis, and was a straight-A student. I couldn't have been more proud of her.

"Still tired?" I asked, handing her a glass of orange juice.

She yawned. "Yeah, but I have a test first period, so I wanted to study a little before I left for school."

I looked at my watch. "Well, you certainly have enough time."

She looked at me like I was dense. "Well, *yeah.* That's why I woke up early."

I shook my head but didn't say anything more. I'd learned recently that you couldn't win an argument with anyone from the age of twelve to seventeen. They knew *everything*.

She took out her history book and began studying while I made her some oatmeal. Then I checked on Max, who'd fallen back asleep watching cartoons, and finally went to my youngest child's room, Jeremy.

"Oh, good you're already up," I said.

He was twelve and had just gotten a new Kindle for his birthday. He now spent most of his time downloading new games or reading science fiction stories.

He pushed up his glasses. "Yes, I just downloaded a new book that's very intriguing. It's about a young boy who is training to become a soldier to fight these bug-like aliens that are threatening his planet. Very intense stuff, mom, you should read it."

I bit back a smile. My son, the intellectual, far beyond his years; he sometimes made me feel like a dolt. "Maybe, let me know how it goes and I'll think about it."

He nodded and returned to his story.

"You have ten minutes and then you should get ready for school, kid," I said, grabbing his dirty clothes hamper.

He nodded. "No worries. I'll be down in a bit."

I stared at Jeremy and was reminded of how fortunate Scott and I were. Both children were intelligent, confident, and fortunately, had their father's sunny good looks.

"You okay, mom?" he asked, biting one of his nails.

I smiled. Of course, he had one of *my* bad habits. "I'm fine. I'll meet you downstairs."

After the kids left for school, I drove Max to the nearby park and started a sizzling, hot detective story I'd just downloaded on my own Kindle, while he played on the slide. The house was clean, the dry-cleaning and laundry taken care of, and my entire day was pretty much free. Since Scott was adamant about me not working and being home for the children when they arrived home from school, I had all the time in the world between the hours of eight and four. I had to admit, though, it made me somewhat jaded at times.

"Hi," said a woman, planting herself on the bench next to mine. She was pregnant and had another child, who appeared to be around four, playing on the jungle gym. She looked to be somewhere in her early twenties, short, blonde bob, pierced nose, and a tattoo of a butterfly on her ankle.

"Hello," I answered, smiling warmly.

"Whew, it's a scorcher today," she said, brushing away the beads of perspiration from her forehead.

I nodded. It was definitely humid. Fortunately, the sun was hidden behind the clouds making it bearable for those of us not pregnant. "You look miserable," I said, noticing her swollen ankles.

"I am and I can't *wait* for this baby to be born," she said, rubbing her tummy. "One month left and I know it won't come soon enough."

"It's tough, I remember those last few weeks."

"They suck, big-time," she said.

I'd packed a small cooler of bottled water and offered her one. "Here, you look like you could use one of these."

She smiled, gratefully. "Thanks, you're a lifesaver. I don't know *what* I was thinking, coming out here without something to drink."

"No, problem," I said, relieved that I'd packed extras.

She tipped the bottle back and guzzled most of it down immediately. Then, she wiped her mouth with the back of her hand and replaced the cap. "I'd better save some for Jenna. That's my daughter."

"Pretty name," I said, handing her another bottle of water. "Just give her this fresh one, I've got plenty."

She looked at me like I was from another planet. "Wow, thanks."

I chuckled. "Hey, like I said, no problem."

She took another sip of water, then pulled out her phone and began texting someone.

Realizing our conversation was over, I started reading my story once again. It was about a sexy cop falling for a suspect that had seduced the *hell* out of him. Some of the scenes were so steamy, that I had to look around to make sure nobody was peering over my shoulder. It was that *intense*.

"Jenna! Be careful!" yelled the pregnant woman. "You might fall!"

I looked up from my story. Jenna and Max were racing around the park, playing tag.

I smiled. "Kids."

She wiped more perspiration from her face with the back of her hand, uncovering an ugly bruise near her eye. It almost looked like someone had smacked her.

I bit the side of my lip, reminding myself that it was none of my business. Instead of meddling, I introduced myself.

"I'm Tina," she answered, rubbing her stomach, again. "So, do you live around here?"

I nodded. "Well, a couple of blocks away. I'm babysitting that little guy and decided to bring him, here to let him get some exercise. What about you?"

She pointed to a group of newer townhomes on the other side of the park. "We live over there."

"That's nice and convenient," I said. "This park has always been one of my favorites. I used to bring my own children here when they were young."

She yawned. "Oh, yeah?"

I nodded. "They keep it pretty maintained, too. Most of the other parks have bird crap on the equipment and graffiti, or overflowing garbage cans; it's gross. This one, though, it's always fairly clean."

"Hmm..." she said, although I could tell she wasn't really impressed.

"Get down, Max!" I yelled, watching him attempt to climb the outside of the covered slide. "You'll fall!"

Tina's cell phone began ringing and she practically jumped off the bench to answer it.

"Hello," she answered, getting up and moving away from me.

I returned to my story, trying not to blush when the detective bent his lover over and frisked her in spots that made me cross my legs.

Good grief, how long had it been since Scott and I'd had sex? Four weeks? Longer?

I looked around again, cleared my throat, and finished reading about the different places Detective stud-muffin buried his smoking gun.

For the love of God...

Now my cheeks were burning, and not from the sun. I turned off the machine and tried to push away the erotic images flitting through my lonely housewife mind. I knew that tomorrow night couldn't come soon, enough. I couldn't even remember the last orgasm I'd had. With the kids getting older and seeming to need more attention than ever, as well as Scott's busy schedule, we barely had enough time for "wham-bam-thank-you-ma'am." The last time that had even occurred seemed like ages ago.

"I just said that I would, Jerry!" hollered Tina into her cell phone.

I glanced her way and noticed the tears in her light blue eyes. When she noticed me staring, she turned away.

"No, I'm sorry," she murmured into the phone. "I'm sorry. Okay?" She swore as she hung up the phone. "Jenna! We have to go!"

"Are you okay?" I asked, seeing the stress and anxiety in her face.

"Husband came home for lunch," she muttered, now trying to avoid eye contact with me altogether.

"Oh. Well, it was certainly nice meeting you," I said.

She nodded. "Yeah, you, too. Come on, Jenna! Your daddy's going to flip out if we don't get home. Let's go!"

Jenna jumped off of the slide and rushed to her mother's side. It was then that I noticed a bruise on the little girl's arm and this time I couldn't stop myself, especially when a child was involved. "Oh, did you get hurt, honey?" I asked, leaning forward on the bench to get a better look.

Jenna looked at her mother. "I –"

"She fell last night," interrupted Tina, grabbing her daughter's hand. "We have a very narrow staircase."

I felt sick to my stomach. Suspicious bruises on both mom and daughter?

Coincidental?

Right.

"Bye, Jenna!" yelled Max.

Jenna turned and waved as Tina pulled her along towards the townhomes.

Max strolled over to my bench and sat down while we watched the two of them leave.

"Did you have fun with Jenna?" I asked, running a hand over his soft hair.

He nodded. "Yes. She doesn't want to go home, though. I wish she could have stayed."

I grabbed his hand and squeezed. "I know, but you might see her again someday."

He looked up at me, his hair flopping over his brown eyes. "No, her dad won't let her. She told me."

I raised my eyebrows. "I'm sure that's not true."

"It is. Just like my dad, they wreck everything."

I sighed. "I know it might feel that way, but your father loves you and thinks he's doing what's best."

He stared at his feet that were dangling off the bench. "He makes my mommy cry. If he loved us, he wouldn't make anyone cry."

I pulled him into my arms. "Sometimes parents make mistakes, honey. It happens to everyone, but that doesn't mean he doesn't love you. In fact, I bet he loves *you* more than anything else in the world."

He frowned. "I heard him tell Anna last night that he loved her beaver more than anything else. I didn't even know she owned a beaver."

Anna was his dad's girlfriend.

Trying to keep a straight face, I cleared my throat. "She must have sold it when she moved in with your dad."

His eyes grew big. "Well, he must miss it a lot then."

I sighed. "No, I'll bet he visits it whenever he can."

Chapter Two

I wanted to treat Max to a healthy lunch, but we ended up at McDonalds anyway for the convenience. After we both pigged out on fries and cheeseburgers, he began yawning.

"Such a big yawn, looks like it's time to go back home and rest until mommy comes to pick you up," I said, grabbing my purse.

He nodded and slid out of the booth. As we were about to leave, we bumped into my hunky neighbor, who was just entering the restaurant.

"Well, hello there, *neighbor*," he said in a rich, deep voice.

I looked up at him and smiled. "Hello there." We hadn't actually met face to face, but he was much taller than I'd originally thought.

"I've been meaning to get your lawnmower back to you," he said.

His statement barely registered as I stared at the ugly stitches near his jawline. As usual, I couldn't stop myself from opening up my big mouth. "Wow, what happened to you?"

He smiled and then winced. "Perks of working in law enforcement, I guess."

"Oh, I didn't know you were a cop. Man, I hope the other guy looks worse than you," I said.

Something flashed through his eyes for a brief second and I thought maybe I'd offended him. I tried to apologize but ended up babbling and sounding like a hopeless idiot. "Oh, God…I'm sorry, I didn't mean that you looked *bad*. I mean you do look bad….the stitches, that is, not you," I cleared my throat. "You're quite handsome."

He chuckled. "Don't worry about it. She doesn't have a scratch on her."

I raised my eyebrows. "A woman did that to you?"

He nodded. "A very *violent* woman with a switchblade. She got lucky and jumped me from behind."

I grimaced. "Wow, I guess it could have been much worse."

"You got that right."

He then looked over at Max and started engaging him in a conversation while I took that time to study him. Not only was he handsome in a rugged kind of way, with his strong five o'clock shadowed chin and eyes the color of warm caramel, but his broad shoulders tapered down to a narrow waist that was very appealing. Being a married woman, one that was starving for sex at the moment, I didn't even dare glance lower.

"Will that work for you?" he asked.

My eyes darted back to his. "I'm sorry, what were you saying?"

As if he knew I was checking him out, his eyes lit up with amusement. "Your husband loaned me the lawnmower. I'll return it tomorrow afternoon, if that's okay?"

I nodded. "No problem."

He held out his hand. "I'm Jake, by the way. Jake Sharp."

"I'm Lindsey Shepard," I said, enjoying the warmth of his hand as well as the size.

Jeez, I must be ovulating.

"Lindsey," whined Max, getting antsy, "let's go."

"Okay, honey. Well, it was nice meeting you, Jake. I'll let Scott know you'll be returning the lawnmower soon."

He smiled. "Sounds good."

We left McDonalds and I brought Max back home with me, putting on a Disney movie so he could relax for a while before Darcy picked him up. Then, I went into the kitchen to sift through my mail when my cell phone began to vibrate.

Darcy.

"Hey, how's it going?" I asked.

She sighed. "It *was* going very well until my Mercedes was towed."

"Shut up!" I gasped.

"Yep, I must not have put enough coins in the meter. Anyway, can you pick me up? I'm still stuck downtown."

"Of course. Max and I will meet you in front of the courthouse, say, twenty minutes?"

"Perfect."

I hung up, grabbed Max and the keys to my SUV.

"Where are we going?" he asked, rubbing his tired eyes.

"Sorry, honey. Your mom needs a ride," I said, buckling him into the car seat.

That woke him up. "Yay, let's go get mommy!"

We sped off and I jumped onto the freeway but noticed, with great dismay, that rush hour had already begun. After sitting in traffic for twenty minutes, I called Darcy.

"Let me guess, rush hour?" she chuckled.

"You got it."

"Don't worry about it; I'm just happy that you're on your way. I'll watch for you, hon; don't fret."

"Okay. I'll see you soon."

When I finally made it downtown, the traffic was still very slow and I had to stop myself several times from swearing at the other drivers. Max had since fallen asleep, thankfully, so I didn't have to answer any more of his "*Are we almost there yet?*" questions.

"Come on," I muttered, trying to maneuver around an old woman who could barely see over the steering wheel. As I turned my head to see if it was safe to pass, I saw Scott moving quickly along the sidewalk, carrying his briefcase. He was alone and entering the Four Seasons Hotel. Knowing they had a very upscale restaurant where he sometimes met his more lucrative clients, I didn't think much about it.

"Mommy!" hollered Max when we finally pulled in front of the courthouse five minutes later.

"Hi, sweetie," said Darcy, getting into the front seat next to me. She put her seatbelt on and turned to look back at him. "I missed you, little man," she said, making a silly face.

He giggled. "I missed you too, silly mommy."

"So, where's your car?" I asked.

"I just spoke to my father. He's picking it up for me," she said. "Three hundred and fifty dollars to get it out, can you believe it?"

I shook my head. "That's nuts."

She sighed and rested her head back against the seat. "At least court went my way. I've got full custody of Max and child support. Frank gets to keep the house, which I didn't want anyway, and his new pet."

"Oh, I bet it's the beaver!" shouted Max from the back seat.

Darcy's eyebrows shot up. "The beaver?"

I laughed. "I'll explain later."

She stretched her arms and put them behind her head. "Anyway, Frank was livid, as you can imagine. But I don't care. He definitely had it coming."

"That's for sure," I said.

My phone started ringing and I looked down at it.

Scott.

"Hey, honey," he said, when I answered. "How's your day going?"

"Okay. How's your day?"

He groaned. "Horrible. I'm at the office, pulling my hair out. I'm sorry, but it looks like it's going to be another long night, I'm afraid."

My heart stopped. I'd just seen him walking into the Four Seasons less than five minutes ago. Why would he tell me he was stuck at the office?

I cleared my throat. "So, you're still at the office?"

He paused. "Yeah."

He was lying and I felt like I'd been kicked in the stomach.

"Okay," I said, trying to remain calm. "I guess I'll see you tonight."

"Babe, are you okay? Your voice sounds funny."

"I'm fine," I said, my lips beginning to tremble.

He sighed. "Okay. Well, I love you."

"Me, too," I answered, trying not to cry as he hung up.

Darcy was staring at me. "What's going on?"

Thinking that I must have mistaken the man walking into the hotel for my husband, I decided to let it go. Scott would *never* have an affair. No way.

I let out a long breath. "Nothing."

Chapter Three

Scott didn't come home until almost midnight, while I stared blindly at my Kindle, waiting for him in our bed.

"Hi, honey," he said, setting his briefcase on the floor.

"Hello."

He loosened his tie and sighed. "Wow, what a long and shitty night."

I cleared my throat. "Did you figure everything out?"

He leaned over the edge of the bed and kissed me on the cheek. "Well, I might have to stop in tomorrow for a couple of hours, just to clear up some loose ends. But then, I'm all yours for the rest of the day."

"Good."

He yawned. "I'm going to take a quick shower. I'll join you soon."

Normally, I wouldn't have thought anything of him taking a shower, but after the episode downtown, him working extremely late, and now the shower, it was disconcerting.

I swallowed a lump in the back of my throat. "Okay."

When I heard the water running in our private bathroom, I scrambled out of bed and grabbed his cell phone, which was in his suit jacket. I checked his *call history*, but found nothing – no previous calls, no text messages. Nothing. He'd apparently erased it all.

Was this normal? Was he in the habit of doing that?

I didn't know. I had never checked his cell phone before, because I'd *always* trusted him.

At that moment, I caught my reflection in our dresser mirror and grimaced at what I'd become. Just because I'd mistaken someone else for my husband, I was acting like some kind of insecure, jealous wife.

Scott loves me.

He told me that every single day. Why would he tell me that if he was seeing someone else?

I sighed with relief. *He wouldn't.*

Feeling paranoid and foolish, I put his phone back and crawled back into bed.

"I feel much better," he murmured into my ear ten minutes later, after sliding in behind me and pulling me close.

"I missed you today," I whispered.

He kissed the side of my neck. "I missed you, too."

We were spooning, and the fact that we hadn't had sex in ages ignited a fire between my legs. I grabbed his hand and placed it on my breast.

He chuckled. "Wow, someone feeling a little frisky?"

"It's been too long. I don't think I can wait until tomorrow," I whispered, turning towards him.

"Then why wait?" He slid his arms around me and began kissing my lips.

I returned his kisses, more fervently than I had in ages, devouring his mouth with mine, tasting the mint from his toothpaste. I was on fire and couldn't get enough.

"I want you, right now," I whispered, moving my hands under his pajamas.

"Wow," he groaned as I began stroking him, turning him from soft to hard. "I guess you *are* horny."

"You don't know the half of it," I said, pushing my underwear down my legs and then kicking them away.

"I'm not complaining," he said,

"Mmm…" I breathed, as his hands moved to my rear, cupping my cheeks and squeezing.

"You feel so good," he whispered as I wrapped my thighs around him and welcomed him inside.

"So do you," I moaned in satisfaction.

He turned until he was on top of me then pulled my nightgown over my head, exposing my breasts, which were, thankfully, still round and firm. "You're so beautiful," he whispered lowering his mouth to my nipples.

I grinned in delight and closed my eyes, meeting his thrusts, reveling in the feel of him inside of me, moving in and out. It felt so good, so filling.

Man, how I'd missed it…

"Touch me," I moaned, now crazy with desire.

He reached down and began stroking between my legs.

"Yes," I moaned, feeling my orgasm begin to build, higher and higher. I wanted it so bad, to feel the release, to scream in ecstasy, to –

"Gonna come," he grunted, then pulled out.

I opened my eyes and looked up at his flushed face.

Seriously?

"Sorry," he smiled sheepishly after he'd finished. He then rolled off of me and sat up.

"Um…it's… okay," I answered, although I felt like someone had shoved a juicy steak with all the fixings in front of my nose, and then emptied it into the garbage disposal.

He brushed his lips against mine, then stood up and went into the bathroom.

I groaned inwardly and then smacked my pillow, knowing it was over. Once he came, he was usually too tired to reciprocate.

Well, there was always tomorrow night...

Chapter Four

I woke up early the next morning and began making breakfast for Scott. I pulled out a mixing bowl and started gathering the items needed for my famous "triple-cheese omelet", which I knew he adored. As I was pouring the egg mixture into the pan, he sauntered into the kitchen.

"Hey, babe," he said.

I glanced over and gave him an appraising look. Today he wore a pair of khaki pants and a light blue polo shirt, which brought out his eyes. His hair was still damp from the shower and I could smell his aftershave, which hinted of sandalwood and cinnamon.

"Hungry?" I asked, motioning towards the pan. "I'm making your favorite omelet."

He stepped closer. "Oh, don't worry about it, Lindsey," he said, squeezing one of my butt cheeks. "Harry's bringing donuts."

I raised my eyebrows. "Donuts? I thought they had too much *gluten*?"

Scott was on some kind of health-food kick and was avoiding anything with white flour. I had to admit, he was looking better than ever. I only wished I had his control. But no, not me – if it was fried, loaded with cheese, or included icing, I was all over it. I guess some would call me a carb whore – I just couldn't get enough.

He laughed and nuzzled my neck. "They do. But after last night, I figured I deserved it."

"Well, save your strength for tonight," I said. "Because you're going to need all the help you can get."

He wiggled his eyebrows. "Sounds like a challenge."

"Oh, it's a threat," I said, handing him a glass of orange juice. "One I think we'll both enjoy. Happy Anniversary, by the way."

"Thank you. Happy Anniversary to you, too," he answered.

"You sure you don't want anything?" I asked, looking down at the pan.

"Sorry, I really don't have time. The sooner I get there, the sooner I can return home," he said, washing out his glass.

"Good," I said.

After he left for work, the kids began waking up and making their way down to the kitchen.

"So, what's on the agenda for today?" I asked Regan as she opened up a container of blueberry yogurt.

She sat down at the counter. "I'm hanging out with Lisa. Isn't today your wedding anniversary?"

I smiled. "Yes. Grandma and Grandpa are throwing a party for us. Make sure you're home by six o'clock, so we're not late."

Jeremy looked up from his Kindle. "Do we *have* to go?"

"Of course you *have* to go," I said. "What kind of question is that?"

"It's just that Hugo invited me over to his house tonight. He has this new video game that I've been dying to try out."

Hugo lives down the street and they've been friends for many years. He has spent as much time at our house as Jeremy has at his. They're practically joined at the hip.

"You're going to have to reschedule that game. I'm sorry, honey."

He frowned. "Well, can Hugo come with us to the party?"

I sighed. "I'll have to ask your father."

"That's not fair, if Hugo gets to come with, then I should be able to invite Lisa, too," pouted Regan.

"We'll see," I said. "Your father and I were planning on spending the night at the hotel while you two went home with your grandparents. I don't think it will work out if your friends tag along."

It was then that I heard someone's cell phone vibrating and noticed that Scott had forgotten his on the counter.

I walked over and picked it up. "Great, your dad's going to need his phone, I'm sure."

Staring at the screen, I noticed that he'd received a text message and that the first few words had flashed across the screen.

I need you…

I frowned. *I NEED YOU?* What exactly was that supposed to mean?

"Mom, can I have some pancakes?" asked Jeremy.

I stared at the phone, its message light blinking as quickly as my heart rate. I was dying to read the rest of the message, but also afraid of what I'd find; especially, after yesterday.

This is stupid, my husband loves me, I reminded myself, once again. We'd just made love a few hours before. It was probably someone at work, waiting for him.

I cringed at my own insecurities. Obviously I'd been watching too many talk shows and they were getting to me. My self-esteem certainly wasn't what it used to me.

"Mom?"

I turned to look at my son. "What?"

Jeremy sighed. "Can I please have some pancakes?"

Scott's cell phone vibrated loudly in my hand, and I dropped it on the counter.

"Good going, mom," snorted Regan. "Dad would kill you if you broke his 'most sacred' cell phone."

"No kidding," I said.

I picked it back up and my breath caught in my throat. It was another message from the same number.

Don't make me wait.

I felt like I was going to be sick. I could barely breathe. This time I didn't hesitate, I opened up his phone and read both messages.

I need you. I'll be waiting in your office.

Second message didn't say anything other than "*Don't make me wait.*"

This could mean so many things, I told myself. *Jesus, Lindsey, don't jump to conclusions.*

I took a deep breath and glanced at my children. "I'm going to dad's office to drop off his phone. I'll be back in an hour, or so."

"I guess that means I'm making my own pancakes?" mumbled Jeremy.

I reached into the freezer and grabbed the frozen ones. "Here, thirty-five seconds in the microwave per pancake. You know where the butter and syrup are." Then I grabbed my keys and purse and left the kitchen.

Trying to remain calm, I opened up the garage door and glanced outside. It wasn't quite ten o'clock and the humidity was back. It certainly didn't help the hysteria that was building inside of me, either. I was a nervous wreck as irrational thoughts started crowding my brain.

Is he cheating?
Would he honestly do that?

I knew one thing, I felt his love. Sure, we hadn't been able to spend a lot of time together, lately, because of his job…

Oh, my God – maybe it wasn't his job keeping him away?!

Choking back a sob, I shoved my keys into the ignition and pulled out of the garage. It was then that I noticed Jake. He was in his yard, bent over the lawnmower, presumably ours, and washing it off with the hose. He wasn't wearing a shirt and his tan, sinewy body glistened in the sun. He noticed me backing out of the driveway and stood up.

"Hey!" he waved and then began jogging over towards me while I tried to compose myself

Crap.

"Are you okay?" he asked a few seconds later, standing outside of my window.

I forced a smile. "I'm fine."

He stared at my face. "You looked like you were panicking there for a second. I just wanted to make sure that you were okay. Prying is a habit of being a cop. I guess."

I should have been a cop.

"It's okay," I answered, not meeting his eyes. "Look, I have some errands to run…"

"I understand. I was just going to ask if it would be okay if I took your lawnmower blade in to the hardware store to get it sharpened. I'll pay for it, of course. It's getting pretty dull."

I turned back to him and forced another smile. "I'm sure Scott will appreciate it. I'll let him know."

"Lindsey, are you sure you're okay?" he asked, frowning.

No, I'm not sure.

"Yes, I'm fine," I answered, trying not to break under his obvious scrutiny.

He nodded and then stood back. "Okay. Well, I guess I'll see you later."

"Bye," I answered and then backed away as he continued to watch me. It was obvious I hadn't fooled him, even though we hardly knew each other. I had a horrible poker face and even my children could tell when I was bluffing.

Scott, on the other hand, was a great negotiator and salesman – qualities that could also make someone a skilled liar, if they were bent on being deceitful. I'd never doubted his honesty in the past, but after the last twenty-four hours, I was beginning to wonder if I was just a gullible wife. I could only hope I was just being a paranoid one.

"I'm probably being stupid," I stated out loud, now speeding towards downtown. "And both of us will laugh about this tonight when we're toasting our anniversary."

I could only hope.

Driving a few miles over the speed limit, I made it to Scott's office building in less than fifteen minutes, and luckily, without a ticket. The security guard, recognizing who I was when I walked through the glass doors, greeted me with a warm smile.

"Hello, Mrs. Shepard."

I smiled. "Hi, Harry. Is Scott upstairs?"

He nodded. "I believe he is. Would you like me to let him know you're coming up?"

I shook my head, vehemently. "It's a surprise," I said. "It's our anniversary and I wanted to give him his gift early."

Great, now I was the one lying.

His eyes crinkled with amusement. "Oh, well happy anniversary."

"Thanks," I answered, feeling rather deceitful myself.

As I stepped onto the elevator, my heart was pounding and my hands were shaking. I was terrified of what I'd find and almost talked myself out of it. When I finally made it to Scott's floor, I stepped off the elevator and walked slowly towards the entrance leading to his advertising agency. Gathering the courage to move forward, I took a deep breath and went in search of my husband.

Chapter Five

The main door to his corporation was unlocked and most of the lights were off, save for the hallway leading towards Scott's office. As I moved hesitantly towards it, I heard a woman's behind me.

"Can I help you?"

I turned around to find an attractive blonde stepping towards me carrying a bottle of champagne. She wore an expensively tailored navy-blue suit, which hugged her perfect body, and heels that showed off slender legs. I could feel the blood rushing to my ears. "I'm here to see my husband," I said in a tight voice.

Her eyes eyebrows shot up. "Scott Shepard?"

I nodded.

She smiled, but there was nothing warm about it. "Well, Scott's in his office. Why don't you go on in and surprise him?"

I nodded, pushed the door open and took a step inside.

"What took you so long?" murmured my husband, who was apparently too enthralled in what was happening in his lap to notice me. "Get over here and join the party."

"What?" I gasped in shock as my brain tried to register what was happening right before my eyes. Scott, loving husband and devoted father, was sprawled out on a black leather sofa, naked from the waist down, while another woman was bent over him, her mouth wrapped around his very delighted penis.

He turned around and his face crumbled right before my eyes. "Shit!" he choked, pushing the other woman away from him. "Wait! Lindsey, this isn't what you think!"

I backed away in horror. "Oh, God...Scott? How could you? How could you do this?!"

He picked up his pants and began pulling them on. "Wait! Lindsey, don't leave, please. I...I can explain!"

"No!" I yelled, moving past the blonde who looked nothing less than amused.

"Lindsey!" hollered Scott.

I ignored the elevator and scurried down the stairs to the parking ramp. By the time I made it to my SUV, I was sobbing so hard, I couldn't even see straight. I got in, covered my face and bawled in misery.

How in the hell could he do this to our family?

Memories flashed through my mind, ones I'd once cherished but now only felt like painful lies. The first time we'd met, the love in his eyes on our wedding day, and the way he'd wept holding our children for the very first time. He'd been everything to me, my very own prince charming; the man of my dreams.

Bastard!

I slammed the side of my fist against the passenger seat several times, wanting to lash out at something, wishing it was his face. Then my cell phone began to ring, startling me back to reality. I grabbed it, knowing before I checked the caller I.D. that it was him. Swearing, I ignored his call and dialed Darcy instead.

"Happy anniversary," she sang into the phone.

"Darcy!" I choked.

She paused. "Lindsey?"

"I need…Scott…he…oh, my God!" I wailed, losing it all over again.

"What happened? Are you okay?"

"Scott…he…" I could barely talk, I was sobbing so hard.

"Honey," she interrupted, her voice cracking. "Where are you?"

"Downtown."

"Okay, okay, calm down and tell me what happened."

I took a deep breath. "Scott… I caught him cheating on me today, just a few seconds ago."

She groaned. "Oh, sweetie, I'm so… sorry. That fucking asshole! It's your *anniversary* for God's sake!"

I wiped my face with the back of my hand. "I know."

"Lindsey, can you drive? Do you want me to come and get you?"

I shook my head. "No," I said. "That's okay. Can…can I come over?"

"Yes, of course. Come over, honey."

"Okay," I sniffed, trying to calm myself down enough to drive. "I'm on my way."

"Be careful on the road. Just remember, I'm here for you. Lindsey, everything's going to be all right. Remember that, sweetie, okay?"

"Mm hmm," I answered, although not really believing it as I hung up the phone. It certainly didn't feel like everything was going to be "okay." All I felt at the moment was pain and insufferable misery.

I jumped in my seat as the ringing of my phone broke the silence.

Scott.

I ignored the fucker and started the engine.

Chapter Six

"You've got to be kidding me," mumbled Darcy, holding my hand as I broke down and told her everything, starting from what I'd seen yesterday.

I shook my head and grabbed a tissue from her coffee table. "No. A woman was giving him head and they were obviously waiting on the other one to join them."

"This is crazy. You have to talk to him. Do you want me to be there with you when you confront him?"

I shook my head, vehemently. "No, I don't want to even talk to that bastard right now! I don't want any explanations or excuses. I just want *him* as far away from *me* as possible."

She sighed. "I don't think that's going to happen the way you want it to. I'll follow you home so you don't have to face Scott by yourself. My mom has Max and I think it would be a good if you weren't alone, especially tonight. In fact, you can either stay here or I'll stay with you at your house."

I nodded. "Thanks. I don't know what to do, Darce," I said as I wiped my face. "What do I tell my kids?"

"If I were you, I wouldn't say anything just yet. Why don't you see if they can stay with friends tonight or have Scott's parents keep them overnight?"

I closed my eyes and groaned. "Crap, I forgot about the party. Just like he apparently forgot he was married. Oh, hell…"

"Well, obviously this party needs to be canceled."

I nodded and blew my nose with another tissue.

She stared out of the window, a pensive look on her face. "When the kids are gone, you should change the locks and pack his shit up. That's what I would do."

I put my head in my hands. "I can't believe this is happening. I've loved him for so long. How could he do this to me?"

She turned back to me and smiled bitterly. "People do crazy things. Seriously, I've known Scott as long as you have and I'd have never guessed he'd do something like this, especially with *two* women? Maybe he has a sex addiction or something."

"Maybe, but it certainly hasn't benefited me if that's the case."

She sighed. "Well, beyond all that, I'm sure he's waiting at home for you right now."

I nodded. "I just don't know how I'm going to face him. I keep picturing that… that… slut going down on him and it's like a knife twisting in my gut."

"Well, you know, you *have* to talk to him. You can't ignore this kind of thing. It has to be addressed."

"I know."

An hour later, Darcy followed me home. Fortunately, my bitterness and tears were now replaced by rage, which gave me the courage to face him. By the time I arrived back at the house, I was so livid I wanted to slash the tires on his Saab, which was now parked in the driveway.

"Ready?" asked Darcy, squeezing my shoulder.

"Yes, I guess so," I said, although I could barely breathe.

She followed me to the porch and before I could get my key into the door, it swung open from the inside.

"Lindsey, thank God," said Scott, reaching for me.

I shot him an evil look as I brushed his hands away and stepped around him.

He sighed and mumbled, "Well, hello Darcy."

"Scott," she replied in a frigid tone.

He closed the door. "Lindsey, please, we obviously need to talk about things. Alone."

I stared at the man I'd been married to for fifteen years and it was as if I was looking at a stranger. Everything I'd been so sure about yesterday morning was now gone.

"Actually," I said, feeling disgusted now that I was face to face with him. "I can't talk about this right now," I said, in a shrill voice. "I want you to pack your stuff and just get the hell out."

He reached for me again, but I stepped back. "Don't be like this, Lindsey. I love *you*. I've always loved *you*. What you saw today had nothing to do with that."

"What?" I barked. "Nothing to do with…have you lost your mind? I'm your wife. Whatever you do affects me, especially, when it comes to… to sex."

Scott glanced at Darcy, again, and then back at me. "I'd appreciate it if we could talk about this, alone. It's hard enough as it is. Please, just give me a few minutes?"

I sighed and looked over at her.

She nodded. "Okay. I'll be in the kitchen if you need me," she glared at Scott. "Sharpening the knives."

Scott shook his head as she walked away but I was glad she'd followed me home. Besides the kids, her friendship was the only thing I was sure about.

"You *had* to bring her along," he said.

"She's the only friend I have at the moment. Now, get on with it," I mumbled, crossing my arms across my chest.

He let out a ragged breath and then reached up and rubbed the back of his neck. "First of all," he said. "I've tried to shield you from all of this, but obviously I need to come clean, about everything."

I snorted. "Obviously."

He pursed his lips. "Lindsey, we're hurting financially. I've been struggling now for the last six months to pay the bills, bring food to the table, Christ, to keep the power going on in the house."

I'd noticed that some of our bills were late, so it didn't surprise me that much. We'd struggled in the past.

"Okay, so we're broke. What does this have to do with you having sex with other women?"

His stared at me. "You realize that my bonuses cover most of our expenses, right? Including this house. Without the bonuses, we'd be living under a bridge."

Our house wasn't luxurious by any means but we were living on his salary alone. That was his choice, however, not mine.

"I still don't understand what this has to do with sex!" I hollered, losing my patience.

He started to pace. "I haven't signed a deal in six months. That means no bonuses, no money coming in."

I was getting so frustrated I wanted to throw him up against the wall. "I repeat, what does that have to do with you getting your dick sucked? Huh? Tell me, because I really don't fucking understand that part of it, Scott!"

He clenched his jaw. "The women that you saw today, they are willing to sign with the firm if I provide… certain services."

"Like sex? You've got to be kidding me," I laughed, bitterly. "You expect me to really believe *that*?"

He sighed. "It's true. If I make them happy…sexually, they've promised to sign with our firm. And Lindsey, they are a huge company. We're talking huge bonuses. Triple digits."

I stared at him in horror. "So, you're doing this for the money? Is that what you're trying to say? You're fucking these two women, for money?"

He sat down on the couch and put his head in his hands. "Yes."

"Look at me," I demanded.

He looked up at me with tears shining in his eyes. Even now, he looked so handsome that it made me want to claw out his face.

"Even if this were true, do you really think I'd be okay with that?" I asked.

"No, of course not."

"How long has this been going on?" I asked.

He shrugged. "The last month or so."

My eyes filled with tears. "You've been screwing around for the last month *or so*?"

"I've been doing this for us. For our family."

I shook my head. "You've been prostituting yourself for the last month. That has nothing to do with me or the kids. I could have gotten a job, or we could have borrowed money from your parents."

He got up and moved towards me. "I love you. I never wanted to hurt you. My only reason for doing this was for us."

I stepped backwards. "That is total bullshit, okay? You should have told them to go to hell. I mean, really – how *could* you possibly think that I'd be okay with any of this?!"

He rubbed the bridge of his nose. "You weren't supposed to find out."

I glared at him. "Obviously!"

He smiled sadly. "The good news is that they told me they'd sign with our company next week."

"Well, kudos to you. Now, I want you to pack your things and get out before the kids return home."

His eyes widened. "You can't really mean that?"

"You're damn right I do. Either you leave or I leave with the kids."

He sighed. "Fine, I'll stay at my parents for now, until you cool down."

I stared at him, incredulously. "Until I cool down?"

He raised his hands. "Okay, until we work things out."

"I hate to say this, but things aren't *just* going to get worked out. I can't trust you, and after walking in on that horrible scene, I don't even want to be near you."

"I'll just give you some time," he said, not really listening to me. "I love you so much. Why can't you believe me?"

"You betrayed us, Scott. Not just me but our children as well. Frankly, I don't know what to believe anymore."

***

Scott called his parents, packed a suitcase, and left. The moment he walked out the door, I started bawling all over again.

"It will be okay," whispered Darcy, hugging me. "You have your friends, your children, and don't forget about your mother. You know how much we all care about you."

My mother.

I groaned.

My zany mother lived in Florida and we talked maybe once a week, which was all I could handle. She lived with her boyfriend, Kyle, who was twenty years her junior, owned a successful botanical shop, and for the last ten years had become a free spirit. Her life now revolved around reading people's auras, spiritual enlightenment, and smoking pot. She claimed that medicinal marijuana helped control her migraines, which had magically appeared around the same time Kyle had stepped into her life. He also suffered from the same type of migraines and had been the one to recommend the therapy.

Go figure.

"I'll call her when things settle down," I mumbled. "If I tell her what's happening, she'll be on the first plane out here."

She tilted her head to the side. "That might not be a bad thing. You need to surround yourself with people who will support you while going through this."

I sighed. "I'll be fine. I just need some time to think about things."

"Just don't give in to whatever crap he's trying to feed you. That talk about having sex to get his deal done, I mean, really? It sounds like a bunch of bullshit."

I bit the side of my lip.

She put her hands on my shoulders and stared into my eyes. "Listen, I know you two have been together for a long time and maybe he still loves you, but you *have* to stay strong. Don't let him manipulate you. What he did is wrong and he knew it every time he stuck his dick inside one of those whores."

I snorted. "He claims it was for us."

"Oh, right, he did it for you and the kids? You know he enjoyed every single disgusting minute of it, and I'm sure he wasn't thinking about you at the time."

"You're right."

"Damn right I am. Now, I've got to get home and pack an overnight bag. We're going to have a girl's night full of male-bashing, good wine, and a large pizza with extra cheese, hold the sausage. Sound good?"

I nodded, although nothing sounded good at the moment. My marriage was over and everything I'd known for the last fifteen years.

What in the hell was I going to do?

What did I tell our children?

"Okay, hon," she said, grabbing her purse. "I'll be back as soon as I can."

When Darcy left, I put a cold rag over my eyes to try and reduce the swelling. Then I made some phone calls and was able to arrange to have the kids stay overnight with their friends. They were both ecstatic about missing our anniversary party and didn't even bother to ask about the change of plans when they returned back home to pack their bags.

"You *rock*, mom," smiled Regan, carrying her new purple and pink skull backpack. "You and dad have fun tonight."

I forced a smile. "Thanks."

"Remember, no drinking and driving," warned Jeremy. "It takes your liver about an hour to metabolize just one ounce of alcohol."

I nodded. "Don't worry; there won't be any drinking and driving. You have my word."

After they left, I started looking through Scott's things. I couldn't help myself. It wasn't until I went into his study and checked the computer that my heart was crushed all over again.

"You bastard," I whispered, looking through his deleted emails, which contained naked pictures of the two women I'd seen earlier that day. Apparently, *they'd* also shared a sexual relationship together and had sent him some pretty raunchy pictures. His enthusiastic replies hammered the final nails into the coffin of what had once been our happy marriage.

I can't wait to have you both.

You make me so horny, I can't see straight.

That certainly didn't sound like a man who was doing this for his family!

I was so angry that I wanted to dump the rest of his belongings out onto the lawn and burn them all to hell. But as much as I contemplated doing it, I knew it would only make *me* look like a bloody fool, so instead, I printed out the emails and shut his computer off. As I was contemplating a more suitable revenge, the doorbell rang.

I wiped away the rest of my tears with the back of my hand and went to answer the door.

Jake.

I stepped onto the porch and his face darkened. "Jesus, did I come at a bad time?" he asked.

I smiled weakly. "No, it's okay."

"I just wanted to bring this over," he said, holding a box. "The delivery guy dropped it off at the wrong house. It looks like it's for Scott. Office supplies or something."

"Thanks," I said as he handed it to me.

He rubbed his chin. "I just have to ask, would you like someone to talk to? I know we've just met, but if you need an ear I'm available."

I sighed. "What I need is my husband, a shotgun, and a shovel."

"Uh oh," he grinned. "Someone's in the doghouse?"

"It's worse than that. He's not even allowed in the doghouse anymore."

Jake leaned against the wood railing and crossed his arms under his chest. "Did you catch him cheating?"

I stared at him in shock. "Yes."

"The only reason I asked is because of his odd schedule and the painful look on your face."

"You noticed it too, huh?"

He nodded. "It's my job to notice things. Plus, I was once a victim myself," he answered with a bitter smile. "I know the signs."

My eyes widened. "You were married?"

"Engaged. My ex-fiancée traveled frequently due to her architectural job. Well, I surprised her one time by showing up at the hotel she was staying at. Needless to say, our engagement ended that night."

I stared at the sexy cop standing less than five feet away and was amazed that anyone would cheat on him. Who in their right mind would give all *that* up?

"Obviously, she was crazy," I blurted out.

Our eyes met and he gave me a grateful smile. "Thanks for saying that. Anyway, I'm just glad I found out before I wasted any more money on the wedding. I almost had to take out a second mortgage just to pay for the damn gown she'd picked out."

"Weddings are expensive. That's why they should only happen once," I said.

"Yeah, well I've since come to the conclusion that marriage isn't for me. I've just recently started dating again, and as far as I'm concerned, it's all I can handle, especially with my work schedule. In fact," he said, pulling out his cell phone, which was vibrating loudly. "Duty calls. I'll talk to you later."

"Okay," I said.

Darcy pulled up as he stepped off my porch to answer his phone. The smile on her face spoke volumes.

"Wow, what's up with super stud?" she whispered. "Don't tell me you're already planning your revenge with the hunky neighbor?"

I grinned, wickedly. "No, but don't give me any ideas."

I then told her about Scott's emails and her lips curled under with disgust. "I tell you what, after hearing that story, I'd definitely *do* your neighbor if I were you. In fact, *do* him until you can't walk the next day. That will get your mind off of the other pain in your ass."

I threw my head back and laughed. "Oh, Darcy, what in the hell would I do without you?"

"You'd lead a dull and boring life, my friend. Now, let's go put this bottle of wine on ice, order a pizza, and cut tiny holes in all of Scott's socks."

Chapter Seven

Darcy tried her best to keep my mind off of Scott, but after drinking two glasses of wine, he was all I could think of. How much I hated him, how much I loved him, how much I wanted to murder him and bury his penis in the back flower garden under a rock.

"He's probably with those whores right now," I slurred.

She pushed her blonde hair behind her ears. "Oh, honey, I'm sure he's at his parents' trying to figure out how he's going to win you back," she said. "He has too much to lose."

I finished my glass of wine and stood up, swaying slightly. "Well, he screwed up. He's already lost me. I'm *never* taking him back."

"Hmm…I think we should skip the last bottle of wine," she chuckled after watching me attempt to open it. "Nothing's worse than a wine headache the next morning."

I waved that ridiculous notion away, removed the cork, and re-filled my glass. "I just can't believe the nerve of that bastard. Here, *I've* been sitting at home like a good little *wife*, pining for him in every way possible, and the entire time he was living it up and screwing not just one woman, but two," I said, holding up my fingers while I tried not to tip over.

Darcy nodded. "He's certainly enjoying his cake."

I snorted. "Cake? He's enjoying his cake and his...his...skank pie!"

She chuckled. "So, how was your sex life the last month when this was going on? Was he coming home and giving it to you, too?"

I choked on my wine.

"Sorry," she said, cringing.

"No, it's okay," I said, clearing my throat. "Well, last night was the first time we'd had sex in over a month."

"Was that normal?"

I shrugged. "Not really, I just thought he was working too much and exhausted. I guess I was right. He was definitely working *hard*. Just not the kind of work I was aware of."

She tapped her long manicured nails on the end table. "Since you're not taking him back, what are you going to do about money?"

"I haven't even thought about that. It sounds like we're already strapped financially."

"Yeah, but you mentioned he's getting a large bonus?"

"Supposedly. But I can't count on him and I'm certainly not asking *him* for anything. Especially now that I know how he earned it."

Her eyes narrowed. "Bullshit, he owes you."

I shook my head. "No, I'm serious about that. I don't want anything from him."

"Well, you'll need to get a job then," she said, leaning back into the sofa.

"I know."

She sighed. "I'm sure you'll find something."

"I hope so, but, honestly, look at me. I'm in my early thirties, I haven't had a job since high school and I certainly don't look like you."

She raised her eyebrows. "Look like me? What does that have to do with anything?"

"You're just so polished and professional looking. Your entire look says 'career woman', my look says, 'housewife'."

She grinned. "Oh, sweetie, we can certainly take care of that."

"Right."

Darcy leaned forward. "Seriously. I'm personally bringing you in to see my hairdresser, and as far as clothing goes, I'll loan you the money until you can pay me back. Problem solved."

"I can't accept that," I said. "It's too much."

"It's *not* too much. Quit being so stubborn and accept my offer. I know you're good with paying me back."

Tears filled my eyes. "Darcy, I don't know what I'd do without you. You're such a good friend."

She squeezed my hand. "Honey, it goes both ways. You've been there for me and I'm just returning the favor. That's what friends do."

"Well," I nodded. "Thank you."

"Now," she said, grabbing the television remote. "Let's watch some sappy movie, gorge ourselves with pizza, and pass out before the clock strikes midnight."

I wiped the tears from my eyes and smiled. "Sounds like our old slumber parties."

She nodded. "Except both of us still believed in prince charming and living happily ever after."

I turned towards the television and sighed. "I won't make that same mistake twice."

Chapter Eight

Darcy left early on Sunday while I shuffled through the house, trying to find ibuprofen for my scorching headache. Finding only one capsule left, I chugged it down with water and tried to rest. Fortunately by the time the kids came home, my headache was somewhat manageable.

"Where's dad?" asked Jeremy while I made them a quick lunch. "Working again?"

I took a deep breath. "Actually, he's staying with grandma and grandpa for a while."

"That's kind of weird, why?" asked Regan.

I smiled, sadly. "Your dad and I are having some issues. We thought it was better if he stayed with his parents for a while."

"What do you mean by *issues*?" asked Regan with a frown. "What kind of problems could you two possibly have? You're like the perfect married couple."

"Everyone has problems," I said. "Although ours is a little too personal to discuss right now."

"Personal? Like as in sexual?" asked Jeremy.

"Oh, God, that's gross," shuddered Regan.

A little surprised by his directness, I said, "The truth of the matter is, we are having problems about *honesty*."

"So, dad lied to you about something?" he asked.

I closed my eyes and rubbed my temples, my headache coming back in full force. "I can't talk about this right now. Let's just say your dad and I are having problems and that it's nothing to concern yourselves with. Both of us love you dearly and this separation has nothing to do with you."

"Separation?" squeaked Regan. "Are you two getting divorced?"

"I really don't know what's going to happen. Just don't worry about it right now, honey, please?"

"They're getting divorced," said Jeremy, matter-of-factly. "Separation almost always leads to divorce between couples. So does infidelity. Mom, did dad cheat on you?"

He's not even thirteen! How in the hell does he know about infidelity and divorce? I wondered, staring at the intellectual Martian disguising himself in my son's body. I chose to ignore his question, however, especially seeing the horrified expression on Regan's face.

I stood up straighter. "As I was saying, it's about honesty, and frankly, I don't know if we are getting divorced. I'm still trying to get a handle on it myself."

"Well…" said Jeremy.

"Kids, let's not worry about it right now, okay?" I said. "Please, just… drop it."

"But," stammered Jeremy.

"Jeremy, enough," I warned. Then I handed them both their sandwiches and escaped out of the kitchen.

"They're getting divorced," echoed Jeremy's voice as I padded down the hallway in my pink fuzzy slippers.

***

Thankfully, Scott stayed away from the house the following week, although he tried calling me several times. When I ignored him, he began calling the kids' phones.

"Dad wants to talk to you," said Jeremy, handing me his cell phone.

Dammit.

"Hello?" I muttered.

"Why aren't you answering your phone?" asked Scott.

I walked into my bedroom and shut the door. "Did it ever occur to you that I didn't answer it because it was *you* on the other end?"

"What, now you're not talking to me?"

"Actually, to be frank, I'd prefer not to."

He sighed. "When can I come home?"

"You're kidding me, right?"

He paused. "This is ridiculous. It's been a week, let me come back."

He sounded like a child. "You honestly don't understand why you can't just come home? Seriously?"

"We went over this and I explained why I did what I did. I know it doesn't make it right, but I was doing it for the family – to keep us off the streets."

I rolled my eyes. "Do you honestly think that's acceptable?"

Or that I'm that naive?

He sighed. "No, but dammit, I love you! And I don't want to lose what we have."

Time to bring out the big guns. "I found the deleted emails."

He didn't say anything.

I tapped my foot angrily, waiting for his response. "Scott, did you hear me?"

He cleared his throat. "What, now you're going through my stuff?"

I laughed, bitterly. "What did you expect?"

"Lindsey, those emails mean nothing. They're just words and pictures."

More lies. Every time I turned around, there seemed to be one more, just hitting me in the face. I wasn't sure what to believe anymore. "Oh, really, is that so? I loved *your* responses, by the way – how horny these women made you, and how you couldn't wait to be with them."

"I know what it says but I didn't mean any of it."

"It's bad enough that I caught you screwing around on me, but the lies – you just can't stop, can you?"

"I love *you*, okay? I made a mistake and I'm willing to put it behind us, if you can."

I groaned. "I can't just sweep this under the carpet, Scott, and I definitely can't forget about it. I mean, Jesus, I walked in and saw it actually happening. It's etched in my mind."

"Counseling, we can go to counseling."

I sighed. "I can't see how a counselor is going to erase the images of your dick in someone else's mouth."

"Just don't give up on us, Lindsey. I love you," he whispered, hoarsely.

"I have to go," I said, feeling like I was about to start crying all over again myself.

"Wait, how about dinner, tomorrow?" he pleaded.

"No. In fact, don't call me for a while. If you want to speak to your kids, that's fine, but I need some space to mull things over. Please respect that."

I hung up before he could tell me any more lies.

Chapter Nine

The following Monday, nine days after I'd kicked Scott out, Darcy decided to intervene.

"You need to get on with life and if you're not going to accept money from Scott, you need to take charge and get a job."

"But…"

"Listen, I made a hair appointment for you. Tonight. Don't argue," she said when I began to protest. "You can always pay me back later."

I sighed. "Okay."

"I'll pick you up around six. We'll get that out of the way and then later in the week, we'll go shop for clothes."

"You know, I just can't thank you enough, Darce."

"You can thank me by introducing me to that hot neighbor of yours, unless you really do have your sights on him," she giggled.

"I've just had my heart ripped to shreds and am not looking to jump into anything, even if it's meaningless sex. Besides, look at me. I'm not exactly *his* type."

"What do you mean?"

I sighed. "I'm not very athletic, I have no style whatsoever, and I'm in a very complicated relationship with my good-for-nothing-but-fucking-other-women, husband."

She burst out laughing. "Bullshit. You're a voluptuous, sexy redhead who could use a giant confidence boost. In fact, he might be able to give you that boost you need."

I snorted. "Right."

"What happened to that confident girl I knew back in high school? The one all the guys were sniffing around."

"I have no idea. I've never met her."

"Oh, that's bullshit. You definitely still have it. You just need to find it, sister."

I sighed. "I'm not really interested in finding anything but a job right now, and a way to cope with all of this crap."

"A little confidence goes a long way and I'm going to try my best to you get there."

I stared at my chipped nails and cringed. "Let me guess, I'm your new project."

"Damn straight. We're going to *ace* this project, too. Just you wait and see."

"Right," I said.

"Have some faith."

"My faith isn't so great these days, so I'll leave that to you."

After hanging up, the kids left for school and I sat on the porch with my mail. As I began sorting through the bills, Jake's front door opened and I watched as he walked a sexy brunette out to her car. He was gloriously naked from the waist up and wore a smile that indicated he'd just gotten laid. When he leaned into her driver's side window and kissed her, I quickly turned away.

This is ridiculous, I thought, feeling a stab of envy. *I'm a married woman.*

As I was trying to sort out my odd reaction, the car pulled away and he went inside, taking his perfectly ripped muscles with him. Fifteen minutes later, he stepped back outside, dressed in his usual running attire, catching my attention once again.

"Hey!" he called out, noticing *me* this time.

I raised my hand and waved back. Then I turned back to my mail.

"Sorry I haven't had a chance to stop over lately to see how you're holding up."

I looked up to find him climbing the steps to my porch.

I shrugged. "I'm doing fine, thank you."

He smiled. "I was just getting ready to run. Do you jog?"

I burst out laughing and motioned towards my body. "Does it look like I run?"

"You obviously keep in shape by doing something. I was just thinking that it would be nice to have someone to run with. It would definitely give me more of a challenge."

"Sorry, but I seriously doubt I'd be a challenge for you."

He grinned. "You'd be surprised."

"Well, I'm busy right now, maybe tomorrow?" I asked.

He nodded. "Okay. I have to work late, tonight, so how about around ten o'clock tomorrow morning? If you're not too busy, that is."

"That's fine. To tell you the truth, I could really use the exercise. I'm not much of a runner, though, so don't expect too much. In fact, I promise that I won't get angry if you leave me in your dust."

"I'd never do that," he laughed.

I smiled. "I'm just saying…"

"I'm sure you'll do fine."

I glanced at his incredibly handsome face, noticing a thin white scar near his eye. It took nothing away from his appearance, if anything making him more appealing in a dangerously sexy way. "The cut near your chin," I pointed, "looks much better."

He nodded. "I heal fairly quickly. Good thing, too," he said, lifting his shirt to show me another scar that went from his navel to somewhere beneath his shorts. "This one looked like a lawnmower attacked me when it happened."

My eyes traveled from his sexy six-pack to his shorts and I could feel my cheeks heat up. "So, um, how did that happen?"

He traced a finger over the scar. "Car accident. Fortunately, I wasn't maimed below the belt."

Fortunately, for the cute brunette, I thought.

"I'd show you the rest, but you'd probably slap me," he said, lowering his shirt with a devilish grin.

I laughed and tried to push the image of him standing naked in front of me out of my mind.

He looked up towards the sky. "I suppose I'd better get going before it gets too hot."

"I hear it's going to be another scorcher."

"Me too," he said. "Well, I'll catch you later, Lindsey."

"Definitely."

Then he was gone, running up the street while I watched with my tongue hanging out. He'd probably spent most of the night pleasuring that other woman and wasn't interested in a drab housewife, but it didn't keep me from enjoying the view from behind.

Sighing, I stood up as my cell phone started ringing again, and frowned. Scott. He just wouldn't give up.

I ignored the call and instead, picked up my mail and went back inside thinking that now might be a good idea to get on the stationary bike; it had been collecting dust for the past five years.

Changing into a pair of shorts and a T-shirt, I glanced at myself in the full-length mirror. I had a little pooch and my bubble-butt certainly wasn't as firm as it used to be. But, when I turned sideways, however, I decided that I didn't look half bad, considering my lack of effort. With a new sense of commitment, I tied my auburn hair back, grabbed a bottle of water, and went to work. Ten minutes later, however, I was huffing and puffing, sweating my ass off and feeling like I was going to die. I began to panic as I thought about tomorrow when I'd be jogging alongside *Captain America*.

Crap, was I in trouble.

Chapter Ten

Darcy arrived to pick me up later that day while the kids sat in the kitchen and worked on their homework.

"Where are you two going?" asked Regan, as she tapped her pencil.

I cleared my throat. "I'm going to get my hair done."

Regan smirked and raised her hands in the air. "There is a God."

"Thanks," I said, pulling one of her blonde locks.

"Mom, even professional stylists don't cut their *own* hair," she said.

"Yeah, *mom*," added Darcy.

"Don't side with her," I warned. "She'll be talking you into getting my legs waxed, next."

"Or bikini line," giggled Darcy.

Catching that statement as he walked by, Jeremy grimaced. "Thanks for that hideous image, Darcy."

Before Darcy could reply, I grabbed her arm and pulled her out of the house, hollering, "See you kids later!"

"You know, now that you're back on the market, you should think about getting a 'Brazilian' down there. Men just love those, in fact…"

I shook my head and got into the car, thankful I couldn't hear the rest of what she was saying.

"Or –," she said, getting into the driver's seat.

I interrupted her. "Enough about my crotch! As far as I'm concerned, I won't be inviting visitors anytime soon."

She started the engine. "Never say never. I'm just saying that it's harder to find a cave when it's obscured by a dense jungle."

I bit back a smile. "You're crazy, you know that?"

She pointed down to her skirt. "Maybe, but you don't need a map to find the entrance to this party."

I sighed. "I hope you find a man soon, you really need to get laid."

She snorted. "You're preaching to the choir, sister."

We arrived at the salon early, so I took a few minutes to glance at the makeup and nail polish displayed in the entryway. Then, when I noticed the prices of Salon Cheveux's haircuts and color options, I cringed; it was definitely *way* out of my budget.

"Excited?" giggled Darcy, when the receptionist called my name.

I smiled and nodded. I *was* actually a little excited about being pampered. It had been too long.

Darcy and I followed a young stylist into the back where she sat me down in her salon chair. The girl's own hair was black with blue highlights, she had tattoos all over her arms, and more piercings on her face than I could possibly count. I was a little nervous but I knew from looking at Darcy that the girl had crazy skills.

"Thanks for fitting her in, Sara," said Darcy. "We both really appreciate it."

She nodded. "You lucked out. I had a cancellation; perfect timing."

"So I'm thinking she could use the *works*," said Darcy.

I stared at myself in the mirror as Sara began running her fingers through my thick, unruly hair.

Sara stared at my reflection intently. "Haircut and some color?"

Darcy nodded. "And those eyebrows need to be shaped."

"Mm…a little bushy, I see what you mean."

"Girls?" I interrupted, my face turning red from their scrutiny.

"Oh, did *you* have some suggestions?" asked Darcy with an amused grin.

I sighed. "Just make me look… sophisticated," I told Sara.

"And sexy," said Darcy.

Sara nodded. "I think we can manage that."

I smiled.

Darcy sat down in the empty chair next to mine to watch. "Okay, Sara, work your magic."

Sara nodded. "I already know exactly what I'm going to do, and believe me – she's going to *love* it!"

Love it? Anything would have to be better than the homemade style I'd walked in with.

Two hours later I stared at myself in the mirror, speechless. I looked like a new woman. My red hair was freshly layered just below my shoulders with foiled copper and blonde highlights. She'd also waxed and plucked my eyebrows, which I had to admit, really brought out my eyes.

"You look amazing," said Darcy.

"She looks drop-dead gorgeous," gushed Sara.

I didn't know about *that,* but I figured I looked much better than when I'd walked in.

"This is also very easy to care for, too," said Sara.

"I'm paying for the hair products, by the way," said Darcy. "You need those, Linds. So, no arguments."

"Thanks. I'll pay you back," I answered. I was beginning to sound like a broken record.

"Just make sure that you come back in a few weeks so we can keep this look going. No more 'do-it-yourself' cuts," said Sara. "Okay?"

I smiled. "Don't worry. I'll definitely be back."

I wasn't sure how I'd scrape up the money, but come hell or high water, I'd be back.

We left the salon with a bag of products that cost almost as much as my hairstyle.

"Now," said Darcy, unlocking her car. "Saturday I'm available if you'd like to go shopping for clothes."

I nodded. "Well, I'm certainly free."

"Good. Have you been looking around for jobs yet?"

"No, I don't even know where to start."

"First of all, you're going to need a resume and then you can check the newspapers and Internet for listings."

I raised my eyebrows. "Resume? There isn't going to be much to list on my resume."

"What kind of computer skills do you have?"

"Actually, I've taken some online classes and can navigate around the Internet pretty well, if I do say so myself."

"Have you used any programs, like Microsoft Word or Excel?"

"Yes, in fact," I said, "I've been working on a book."

She stared at me. "A book? What do you mean?"

I shrugged. "Just a story I've been working on for quite a while. It's more of a hobby, though."

"Well, you always were a good writer, even back in high school," she said. "What is it? Romance, horror, mystery?"

"Actually, it has a little of everything."

She smiled. "Can I read it?"

I bit my lower lip. "Maybe…"

"Seriously, email it to me so I can read it."

I nodded. "Okay, but just remember I'm only a rookie. Don't expect too much."

She shook her head. "You have absolutely no self-confidence, do you? I have a feeling that's going to change now that you've booted Scott to the curb permanently."

"What do you mean?"

She raised her eyebrows. "Oh, come on – he basically controlled your life! Kept you from working, didn't allow you to get out there and spread your wings. Remember back in high school? You had so many dreams."

I sighed. "He never stopped me from doing anything. I just became pregnant and things turned out differently. I'm happy with my life, though. Or, I was."

She reached over and squeezed my hand. "Well, now things have turned out differently for you yet again. Everything happens for a reason, Linds, and I have a feeling you've turned a corner in your life that's going to open up more possibilities than you could have ever imagined."

"I wish I had that same optimism," I murmured.

She smiled. "You just wait. Your life's not over, it's just changed course and headed towards a whole new adventure."

Before I could respond, she slammed on the brakes.

"Shit!" she hollered staring at a pregnant woman who'd sped out of the darkness and was now standing in front of the car, flagging us down.

"What in the hell is that woman doing?" barked Darcy.

As the stranger moved closer I recognized her as Tina, the young woman I'd met at the park over a week ago.

"Do you need some help?" I asked, rolling down the window.

"Yes, please help me!" she sobbed, her face a mess of mascara and tears.

Darcy unlocked the back door and the woman jumped in. "Do you need a doctor or the police?" she asked.

She pointed. "Oh, God, here he comes! Get us the hell out of here!" cried Tina.

We both turned towards a tall young man rushing towards us. He wore a police uniform and a look of utter dismay.

Darcy turned towards the panic-stricken woman. "Why in the world are you're running from a cop? What the hell is going on here?"

"He's my husband! Please, we have to leave!" shrieked Tina.

But the man was holding his hands up defensively and already blocking our path. "Tina, honey," he said, moving towards my side of the car. "Baby, *what* are you doing?"

Tina didn't answer.

He smiled at me and Darcy apologetically. "I'm terribly sorry; my wife is pregnant and gets a little… emotional."

Darcy's eyes narrowed as she turned back towards Tina. "Are you okay? Would you like us to take you somewhere else to talk?"

I looked at Tina, whose eyes were now locked with her husband's. As they stared at each other, you could cut the tension with a knife.

Darcy and I glanced at each other, not sure what to do.

The man smiled coldly at his wife and the look in his eyes even gave me the chills. "Come on, honey," he said, evenly. "Jenna really needs you. She's frightened."

Tina drew in a sharp breath and opened the door.

"I knew you'd see it my way," he said with a smug look on his face.

"Wait, Tina!" I called as she began moving back towards her home. "Can you come here just for a minute, please?"

She walked back to my window and bent down, a despairing look on her face. "Yeah?"

I whispered my address and she nodded, slowly. I reached for her hand and squeezed it. "Seriously, *don't* forget it. I'm so close and very willing to help, if you need it. You and Jenna."

"Tina, let's go," commanded her husband.

Without answering, Tina turned away and we watched as she followed him back into their townhouse.

"What in the hell just happened there?" asked Darcy. "Did we make a mistake by letting her go back in there?"

I rolled up my window. "Considering the fact that I saw bruises on her face the other day, I think she definitely needs some kind of help."

"Shouldn't we call the police?"

I sighed. "Honestly, I don't know what to do. We can't prove anything and she went back with him willingly."

"Maybe you should run it by your next door neighbor? He's some kind of cop, right?"

I nodded. "You know, that's a very good idea."

Chapter Eleven

After Darcy dropped me off in front of my house, I went inside to let the kids know I'd returned.

"Holy crap, mom!" laughed Regan. "You look so much better."

"Watch the language," I answered, smiling in spite of myself.

Jeremy frowned. "You really are getting divorced, aren't you?"

I sat down next to him on the sofa. "To be honest, honey, I really don't know."

"Well, when Hugo's mom got divorced, she lost weight, bought a Humvee *and* a giant set of hooters. Now she has two or three boyfriends and he hardly ever sees her."

Regan rolled her eyes. "Hooters? You're so gross."

"What? It's true," he said.

I smiled. "I assure you, that won't happen, here."

Both of them looked at me as if they didn't quite believe me.

I raised my eyebrows. "Look, the only reason I had my hair done was because I need to find a job. Your father and I could really use the extra income right now."

"A job?" asked Jeremy. "I thought dad made decent money?"

"Things are tough right now, even for him," I said.

Just then, my cell phone started ringing. I grabbed it out of my purse and groaned inwardly.

Scott.

Shoving it back into my purse, I noticed it was almost nine o'clock. "You both should get ready for bed. You have school tomorrow."

"Fine. By the way, dad called for you, *again*," said Regan. "You're supposed to call him back."

"I'll take care of it," I said. "Now, take a shower and get ready for bed."

After the kids were settled in for the night, I looked out the window and noticed that Jake still wasn't home from work, so I decided to wait for him on my porch. I grabbed my Kindle and a blanket then settled into my glider bench and began reading the rest of my sensual detective story. Soon my eyelids grew heavy and I dozed off.

The sound of thunder woke me up some time later and I was slightly irritated. I'd been in the midst of an erotic dream, my faceless lover devouring my skin with kisses, driving me wild. I wanted more, and oh… he was about to give it, I could just sense it. But then I was ripped from the dream and forced back to reality.

Dammit. Even my dreams leave me sexually frustrated.

Sighing, I pulled my blanket in closer and watched as thick raindrops began to fall onto the steps, wondering if I should just go inside. But then, Jake's unmarked sedan pulled up to his driveway as the rain began to pour.

I got up, put my blanket and Kindle back inside, and rushed over to his garage through the rain, where he was grabbing a beer from a small refrigerator.

"Jake?"

He turned around and stared at me. "Oh, hey, Lindsey."

"Sorry to bother you," I said, shivering slightly from my wet clothes. "I…um…there was an incident today and my friend suggested I talk to you about it. You mentioned you were a cop, right?"

"I'm actually a Narcotics Detective." His eyes narrowed. "What's going on, did Scott do something?"

I shook my head. "No, nothing like that." I then explained what had happened earlier with Tina while he listened.

He sighed. "Well, I could check it out if you think she's in any real danger."

"I definitely believe she's being abused; there were bruises on her face and also on her child the other day at the park."

He frowned and then put his beer back into the fridge. "Want to take a ride?"

I nodded.

He motioned for me to get into his car and then joined me. As we were backing away, he glanced at my shirt and smiled. "Chilly?"

I looked down and my cheeks grew hot. My T-shirt was wet, and through my bra you could see that my nipples were at full attention. I crossed my arms over my chest. "Damn rain."

He chuckled and turned on the heat. "I certainly didn't mean to embarrass you."

I sighed. "No, it's fine," I said, dying to change the subject. "Anyway, Tina lives near the park, by the newly constructed townhomes."

Our eyes met. "You said he was a police officer?"

I nodded. "Yes, but he certainly didn't look like he was ready to protect and serve."

He chuckled. "Well, I'll check it out while you wait in the car."

"Okay. Thanks again, Jake."

"No problem."

As we drove near Tina's, I could smell a trace of his cologne, a slight woodsy scent. It made him even more appealing and I groaned inwardly at my growing attraction towards him.

What the hell was wrong with me? I wondered, laying my head back against the seat. *Was I turning into one of those lonely, desperate housewives? Would I be hitting on the pizza man or the cable guy, next?*

"You okay?" he asked.

Our eyes met again. "I'm fine."

"We'll get this figured out," he said. "I'm pretty good at reading people. If she's hiding something, I'll know within the first thirty seconds. Then we'll go from there."

"Okay."

Tina's house was dark and quiet by the time we pulled into her driveway.

"Lindsey," said Jake, "you wait right here. I'll be back."

I nodded and watched as he approached the house in the rain, knocking on the door. A minute later, the husband answered and Jake pulled out his badge. They spoke for a while and then Jake followed him inside.

I stared at the house and noticed a little face peeking out of an upstairs window.

Jenna.

She ducked away and my stomach tightened with worry. How could anyone hurt a child –

especially, a cop? I could only pray that Jake's appearance would knock some sense into Jerry, or that Tina would come to *her* senses and tell Jake the truth. Deep down I knew it wasn't that easy.

Ten minutes later, it had stopped raining and Jake stepped back outside, still talking to Jerry. When they were finished, Jake turned and began walking back towards the car as Jerry watched. When he saw me in the passenger side, recognition spread across his face. He waved at me with an eerie smile and I felt a cold shiver run down my spine.

Jake got in and closed the door. "Well, I spoke to Tina and her husband, Jerry. Even checked on their daughter and everything seems calm at the moment. Tina claims it was her hormones that started the fight earlier."

I frowned. "She's scared of him."

He sighed. "Personally, I felt something a little off, too. Unfortunately, there's nothing more we can do, right now. I was actually surprised that he let me in."

I stared out the window. "He's a cop. He probably doesn't want any trouble."

"Of course not."

I sighed. "So, let me get this straight, unless she turns up missing or dead, we can't do anything else to help her?"

"Not much, but you could call Child Protective Services and let them know you saw bruises on the little girl. They might be able to do something."

"I hope so."

We drove home in silence until he pulled into his driveway. "So, are you ready for our run tomorrow?" he asked, shutting off the engine.

"I hope so."

His eyes glittered in the darkness as he smiled. "Well, don't worry. I'll go easy on you."

"Like I said, don't let me hold *you* back. My pace and yours will be slightly different."

"You're underestimating yourself or overestimating me."

"Yeah, right," I said, opening the door. All this talk about our bodies moving together was making me warm and I definitely needed some cool, fresh air.

He got out and cleared his throat. "I'll walk you to your door. It's pretty dark."

Our neighborhood was as safe as any, but after seeing the cold look in Jerry's eyes, I welcomed Jake's offer. "Okay, thanks."

"So, how are *you* doing?" he asked as we walked to the end of the driveway. "You certainly appear happier than the last time we talked. Your hair looks very nice, by the way."

I touched my hair, which was still wet from the rain and couldn't have looked very appealing at the moment. I smiled. "Thanks. I'm still pretty devastated, but after this thing with Tina, I'm just grateful my kids and I are safe and not living in *fear* of their father."

His lips thinned. "It's a crazy world. There's so much shit going on all around us, you have no idea. Things I've seen that will probably haunt me for the rest of my life. Fuck, I had no clue what I was getting myself into when I signed up for this job."

I frowned. "It has to be really tough."

He sighed and ran a hand through his dark hair. "Yeah, well I shouldn't burden you with my problems. Sorry."

I touched his forearm. "No, don't worry about it. Everyone needs a friend or someone to talk to."

He smiled. "That goes both ways, I hope you know."

I smiled back. "Thanks."

"Well," he said as we stepped onto the porch. "Get some sleep. I'll be over around ten, is that okay?"

I nodded.

He stared at me quietly for a minute, then reached over and brushed a strand of hair from my lips. "You're husband's an idiot," he stated.

"Thanks," I answered, reminding myself to breathe.

He nodded and stepped back. "Well, I'll see you tomorrow, then?"

"Sure will. Goodnight, Jake."

"Goodnight."

I closed the door, thinking about the way he'd looked into my eyes. He'd definitely caused my pulse to race, which was really frustrating. I didn't want to be attracted to him or anyone else at the moment. Including my husband.

"Where've you been?"

"Scott?" I gasped, turning on the light in the living room. "Jesus, what are you doing sitting in the dark?"

He was lounging on the sofa with his tie undone, holding a glass of scotch. From the look in his eyes, it wasn't his first. He twirled the half-filled glass in his hands. "I came home to talk to my wife, who keeps avoiding me."

"We've already talked," I said. "I told you before that I need some time to figure things out."

He stared at my hair and smirked. "Looks like you've already figured things out – a new hairstyle, rendezvousing in the middle of the night with the single neighbor; tell me, has he made his move yet?"

I stared at him incredulously. "First of all, *you* have no right making accusations. You're the one who's been screwing around, not me, so don't even go there!" I snapped.

"So you're getting even now?" he asked sourly.

"You're pathetic," I said, "and you need to leave."

He stood up and moved towards me, a threatening look in his eyes. "*This* is my home and *you* are my wife. I'm not leaving."

I stared at him with something close to fear, a feeling I'd never felt towards him in all of our years of marriage. "I'm not going to tell you again," I said in a strangled voice. "You need to leave."

His face softened. "Would you just stop this?" he said, trying to reach for me. "For God's sake, Lindsey, I love you. Doesn't that mean anything to you?"

I pushed him away and moved across the room. "It *did* mean something. In fact, it meant everything to me. But the things that you've done," I said, my eyes filling with tears, "those things also mean something."

"I made a mistake," he said, swaying slightly. "I know. But I can't change what happened. Just please, can't you give me another chance?"

"If you're looking for another chance, this isn't the way to do it. You've obviously been drinking too much and now you're trying to bully me into letting you back into my life? Seriously?"

Tears rolled down his face. "I'm sorry. I just need you so much."

I raised my hand. "Stop, okay. Scott, you can sleep in the guest room tonight, but you'll need to leave early in the morning. The last thing we need is you getting thrown in jail for drinking and driving."

He ran a hand through his hair and stared at me with a look of defeat. "Fine, I'll leave you alone tonight. But don't think for one second that I've given up. I'm not letting you go that easily."

You already let me go when you cheated on me, I thought as I watched him stumble towards the guest room.

Chapter Twelve

Thankfully, Scott was gone by the time I woke up the following morning. The children had also missed seeing him, so there wasn't any explaining to do.

"See you tonight," I said as they both took off to catch the bus. Jeremy was still eyeing my new hairstyle with trepidation.

I sighed. "Jeremy, what's wrong?"

He just shook his head and walked out the door.

I decided that I needed to talk to him again when school was over. He was obviously very concerned and I couldn't blame him one bit. I only wish I had a straight answer for him. I wasn't even certain of what was going to happen.

Sighing, I went into the bathroom and looked in the mirror. I cringed at my reflection and decided to take a shower before the run so I could shave my legs to avoid any embarrassing stretching moments. Then I put on some shorts, pulled my hair into a ponytail, and dug out my tennis shoes.

You can do this, I told myself, taking one final glance in the mirror. So my body wasn't as toned as I would have liked and I avoided wearing shorts even in the hottest of weather. I was a mother and had labored for over thirty-six hours of excruciating pain and agony giving birth to Regan. I'd suffered pain that would have brought most men to their knees. Not only that, I'd survived and had repeated the process all over with Jeremy. Run a few blocks?

Hell yeah.
Bring it on.

***

It was shortly before ten when I walked over to Jake's house with my bottle of water. He was in the garage, putting away some tools.

"Hey there," he said, closing his tool chest.

I smiled. "Hey there yourself."

He stepped outside and closed the garage. "So, did you get a good night's sleep?"

I shrugged. "It was okay."

He tilted his head. "I noticed Scott leaving early this morning. Everything okay?"

"He was in the house when I returned home last night. He'd had a little too much to drink and I told him to stay in the guest room."

"Let me guess, he wants to make things right?"

"Of course."

"What do you want?" he asked, stretching his calves. Today he wore blue shorts and a snug white T-shirt that, as usual, emphasized his incredibly sexy body.

I pulled my eyes off of his pecs and followed his lead, stretching my lily-white legs. "To be honest, I really don't know. I'm disgusted with Scott's actions and the idea of having to learn how to trust him makes me so damn angry. I shouldn't have been put into this situation. Not by my own husband."

"Very true."

"He keeps telling me how much he loves me. It just seems like bullshit to me, though, especially after screwing those other women. If he loved me, he should have been able to control himself."

He stretched one of his arms behind his neck. "Love and lust are two separate things, although there are times when you can't control either."

I bent down to stretch my other leg, causing my eyes to be in direct line with his crotch. I turned away and tried to focus on my stretches.

"Hungry?"

Our eyes met and the smile he gave me had me wondering if he sensed my impure thoughts.

"What do you mean?" I asked, my cheeks burning.

He laughed. "I was just thinking that we could jog up to that little coffee shop on Grande Avenue for a quick bite to eat as a reward. My treat."

I nodded. "Sounds great. I think I might actually be able to handle that distance."

Man, was I ever wrong. After about five blocks, I was huffing and puffing so hard, we had to stop.

"You okay?" he asked, while I bent down, gasping for dear life.

"I'm… so… out of shape," I said through wheezes. "Sorry."

He smiled. "Don't be. Everyone, no matter what kind of shape they're in, has to start somewhere. It takes a while to build up stamina."

I closed my eyes and imagined his stamina was very, very, good. "Some more than others," I said.

"Don't worry; you're just not used to it. It *will* get easier."

I wiped the sweat from my forehead. "Look, why don't you just go ahead of me and I'll catch up, eventually."

He shook his head. "No, we can just walk. This was my idea and I'm not going to leave you."

"Thanks," I said after chugging back most of my water. "But I won't take it personally if you decide to start running again. Honestly."

"Right now, I'd rather walk, with you."

I couldn't help but smile. "Okay."

We talked about our families as we walked into town. He'd lived in Minnesota prior to moving to Texas, and his relatives were all deceased.

"That must be difficult," I said. "Not having anyone left."

He sighed. "This might sound cold, but it's actually been a lot easier, especially since my mom passed away a few years ago."

"Really?"

He stared ahead. "I usually don't talk about this but…she spent most of her life battling a Heroin addiction. In fact, I was taken from her when I was twelve."

I stopped in my tracks and touched his arm. "Seriously? Where did you go?"

He shrugged. "I was transferred around from home to home. I was an angry kid and I guess you could say, not very easy to control."

"But you were young and I'm sure you had every right to be angry."

He stared at me for a minute and smiled. "It wasn't easy, that's for sure."

"Well, you've obviously come a long way since then."

He took a drink of water and wiped his mouth. "There was some counseling involved.

Then, after I was reunited with my mom and saw how much she'd lost in life, it gave me the incentive to do better."

"Did she stop using?"

His lips tightened. "She was in and out of rehab more times than I could count. In the end, she didn't have the strength to stop for good."

"Did she die because of the Heroin?"

He nodded. "She overdosed."

"Wow, I'm sorry," I said softly.

"Don't feel pity for me. In fact, I guess you could say that shit only made me stronger."

"I can imagine," I said.

"It's what also led me into criminal justice. Getting rid of the poison on the streets is what keeps me going back to work every night, even when the shit is so utterly fucked up…" He stopped talking and shook his head. "I'm sorry."

I raised my eyebrows. "For what?"

"For venting when you already have enough things to think about."

I stopped walking. "Are you kidding me? I'm happy that you're opening up. It helps a person get through stress, having someone else to talk to."

He tilted his head and smiled. "Well, I appreciate you lending an ear."

"That goes both ways," I said.

"Good. Because I enjoy helping 'damsels in distress.'"

I laughed. "Damsels? Is that what I am?"

"Definitely. I spent many years being a hell-raising punk and now I'm determined to be a good guy, no matter how boring it is."

"Oh, now good is boring?" I asked.

"Even you have to admit that being bad is a hell of a lot more fun."

"I don't know, I've been a good girl most of my life, except for when I was in high school and used to sneak out for parties."

"That long ago, huh?" he said, looking amused. "Well, we should fix that."

I laughed. "Is that so?"

He nodded. "Yeah. In fact, I'm going to mull over this for a while and get back to you."

"Let me guess this straight…you're going to think of ways for *me* to be bad?"

He smiled darkly. "Believe me, the idea probably excites me more than you. And of course I mean that in a strictly platonic way."

"Wow," I chuckled. "I don't even know what to say."

"You'll be saying 'thank you' once I'm finished. By the way, you can still be bad and do it legally; just so you know."

"Oh, I know," I said, glancing at him out of the corner of my eye. I knew there were many ways to be bad, but at the moment I wasn't thinking of anything 'platonic.'

"So," I said, changing the subject before my dirty little mind worked overtime. "You never mentioned your dad."

"My dad," he laughed bitterly. "The asshole is probably alive, but I don't know for sure. He was one of my mom's 'Johns'."

I cringed. "Oh."

He shrugged. "I've learned to accept it and not blame her. She was at the mercy of the drug and did what she could for money. I guess you could say that my mom, my dad, and I were all victims of Heroin."

"Ain't that the truth," I said.

"Okay, now that you know my life history, what about you? Are your parents alive?"

I told him about my hippy, free-spirited mom, and her younger boyfriend.

"Well, she sounds pretty cool, actually."

"She's definitely not your typical fifty-five-year-old. In fact, I guess you could say that growing up she was more like a sister than an actual mother."

"Was that bad?"

"Most of the time it wasn't. But, there were times I definitely needed a mother and she didn't mature to that point until I found out I was pregnant at eighteen. Then she blamed herself for not being strict enough and changed her parenting ways."

"What do you mean?"

"She became a strict overly-protective mom to my younger sister, Caroline."

"How'd that go for your sister?"

I smiled. "She complained about it constantly, but she ended up going to college and marrying a doctor. I suppose they have a good life, although we don't talk much, anymore."

"Why?"

"Lots of reasons, the main one being Scott. She never cared for him."

"*Now* might be a good time to catch up with her, then."

"I don't know, I just hate dragging my family into my problems."

"I can understand that. That's why it also helps having good friends."

I nodded. "Yes, it does. So, the holidays are coming up. Where do you spend your holidays without family?"

"I still have plenty of friends," he answered. "I try not to impose but if they ask me over for dinner, I'm certainly not going to refuse," he said, smiling sheepishly. "I'm a lousy cook myself."

"Well, next holiday, if you aren't busy, you're welcome to join my family."

He chuckled. "I'm sure Scott would just *love* that."

"Truthfully, I'm beginning to doubt that Scott will even be invited back," I answered.

"Well, I hope everything works out for the best, whatever it is. You deserve it."

I smiled. "Thanks."

When we finally made it to the coffee shop, both of us ordered ours black and over ice, then sat down to enjoy a couple of blueberry scones.

"These are really good," I said between bites. "But I think I'm defeating the purpose of trying to lose weight. These have to be filled with mucho calories."

He shrugged. "You look great. Forget about losing weight and focus on feeling good. Tell you what, if you keep getting your heart rate up every day for at least twenty minutes, you won't need to worry so much about watching calories."

"Well, to be totally serious with you, I'm not much into running. I don't know how long I'll be able to keep this going."

"There are other ways to get your heart rate up. Biking, aerobics, walking," he grinned, wickedly. "Even sex."

I snorted. "Well, if Scott's moving out permanently, I can count that particular exercise out, too."

"You're a beautiful and sexy woman. I'm sure that you'll find plenty of willing partners."

"Right," I said, blushing.

He rubbed his chin and smiled. "That's another thing that fascinates me about you. You're so unassuming and unaware of your effect on men, it's refreshing."

I burst out laughing. "My effect on men?"

"You haven't noticed the way some of these guys in this shop have been eyeing you?" he asked, finishing his coffee.

I raised my eyebrows and looked around, not really seeing it, myself. "You're kidding, right?"

"See, that's exactly what I mean. Not only are you modest, but you're unpretentious."

I put my hand to my cheek. "Stop, sir, you're making me blush, *again*," I teased. "And I'm much too old for that."

"Yeah, you're *so* old. What are you, early thirties?"

I laughed. "You *were* on a roll, why didn't you say twenties?"

"Because we're friends, and I'm not trying to feed you a line of bullshit. Obviously, with two children in their teens, you're probably not in your twenties."

"Okay, I'm thirty-three. What about you?"

"Me? I'm thirty-five. Anyway, my point is that you're still young and even though you're going through some tough shit right now, keep your chin up. Don't let anyone, including your husband, take advantage of you. Life is much too short."

I nodded, knowing what he said made perfect sense. It just wasn't an easy option for me, however, especially having two confused children and bills that I couldn't possibly pay on my own.

His phone began to vibrate. "Shit, I'd better take this," he said, checking the caller I.D.

I stood up. "I have to stop into the bathroom, anyway. Meet me outside?"

He nodded and grabbed our empty cups.

When I was finished in the ladies' room, I met Jake back outside and he seemed agitated.

"I have to get moving – quickly," he said. "Some shit at work. I'm sorry."

I waved my hand. "Oh, Jesus…no problem at all. Why don't you run back and I'll take my time? I might just do a little window shopping at some of the shops around here anyway."

He swore under his breath. "I'm really sorry about this. Are you sure?"

"Of course, I have nowhere to go and you obviously do, so you should go."

"Thanks," he said, and then before I could respond, he bent down and planted a warm kiss on my cheek. "That's for being such a kick-ass neighbor as well as a good listener."

"Well, you're welcome," I answered, unable to wipe the grin from my face.

"You know, I was planning on picking up a couple of steaks on the way home from work Friday night, maybe do some grilling. It wouldn't be until after nine, but are you interested in joining me for a late meal? It gets a little lonely eating alone all the time, you know?"

I wondered about the pretty brunette again. *Obviously*, she'd been invited over for more than a just a plate of food. But Jake and I were just getting to be good friends. "Sure. I'd be happy to keep you company."

"Great. Second question, join me again tomorrow?"

I grimaced. "I don't know… I mean, I'll just slow you down again."

He snorted "Don't worry about it. I enjoy the company."

I nodded slowly. "Okay; same time tomorrow?"

"You bet, unless more shit comes up at work," he said, motioning towards his cell phone.

"Right, well, I guess I'll see you then."

Chapter Thirteen

I took my time going back home and even passed by Tina's place to see if she was around and wanted someone to confide in. Unfortunately, she wasn't but her husband was outside, mowing the lawn and he recognized me right away.

"Well, well...look who it is," he said, shutting off the lawnmower. "Tina's new little buddy."

I ignored him and kept walking, angry at myself for even choosing that particular route home.

He sauntered towards me, taking a swig from a bottle of beer. "You'd best keep on walking, you nosy little bitch, if you know what's good for you."

I stopped and glared at him, unable to help myself. "You know, it's sure a pity."

He smiled coldly. "What's a pity?"

"It's a pity that a woman is beaten by someone who's supposed to uphold the law and keep everyone safe. It's even more of a pity that a grown man would use his fists not only on his pregnant wife, but also his little girl."

His lips curled into a scowl. "You don't know what you're talking about, you cunt."

I glared at him. "I think I do, and I certainly know a coward when I see one."

His face turned red and he took another step closer to me. "You know who you're messing with, bitch?"

"You don't scare me," I said, raising my cell phone. "And *I'm* certainly not afraid to call for help."

His nostrils flared. "You should get the hell away from my property."

I pointed at him. "And you should keep your fists off of your wife."

We stared at each other with mutual hatred until I pulled myself out of it and began walking away.

"That's right, you should be scared, Lindsey!" he hollered. "And don't forget to lock your doors, especially at night. Keep out the boogieman!"

I froze and turned around to face him, wondering how the hell he knew my name.

He finished the rest of his beer and smiled. "Bye, now."

***

By the time I made it home, I was nauseated and shaking, but not from running. I decided to tell

Jake about the confrontation with Jerry as soon as he came home. It certainly troubled me that he'd found out my name and hinted at knowing where I lived.

Locking my doors, I grabbed some clean clothes and jumped into the shower. When I was done, I noticed that Darcy had left me a message to call her back.

"Hi, lady," she said. "Just calling to see if you received my little gift in the mail yet?"

I raised my eyebrows. "Little gift?"

She sighed. "Guess you haven't."

I narrowed my eyes. "What exactly did you do this time?"

"It's a surprise and you'll just have to wait," she teased.

"A surprise? You have to quit spoiling me like this."

"You're my best friend, for God's sake. Someone's has to look out for you."

I smiled. "Well, thank you."

"So, did you talk to Jake about the woman we almost ran down last night?"

I told her what had happened, including my most recent episode with Jerry.

"That son-of-a-bitch," she snapped. "I think you should report that."

"It's my word against his and really, nothing happened."

"Well, tell Jake and keep your doors locked at night. This guy sounds like a real asshole."

Thinking about him prowling around near my house in the middle of the night gave me goose bumps. "Oh, I will."

"Shit, it's getting late and I'd better get back to work. Now, don't forget about Saturday."

Shopping.

I smiled. "Thanks, Darcy. I'll pay you back as soon as I can."

"I'm not worried about it. I also might have some leads on a couple of jobs. I'll email you the information to see if you're interested."

"Okay, thanks," I said.

"Call me later, okay?"

"Sure, talk to you soon."

After I hung up, I cleaned up around the house and took out the garbage. Two hours later, I noticed Jake's car pull in to his driveway. I immediately went over and told him what happened.

His jaw clenched tightly as I finished the story. "I think he needs a reminder of who *he's* messing with," he growled.

"I'm sure it was all talk, but I have to admit, it freaked me out."

"Don't worry about this, Lindsey. I'll take care of it," he said, preparing to leave.

I raised my hand. "Wait, I don't want this to turn into something worse than what it already is. I mean, it was just words."

He shook his head. "He's a police officer. He shouldn't be threatening anyone, let alone defenseless women and children. Now he's trying to frighten you? That's bullshit."

"Please," I said. "I don't want him to know he made me nervous. If you go over there, he's going to think he's won. I think a guy like that gets off on scaring people and I don't want to give him the satisfaction."

He stared at me for a few seconds and then let out an exasperated breath. "Fine. But if he gives you any trouble, let me know."

I nodded.

"Can I see your cell phone?"

I took it out of my pocket and handed it to him.

"Here's my number," he said, adding it to my contact list. "Call me, day or night. I don't care."

I smiled. "Thanks, Jake."

His eyes softened. "No problem."

Just then, a FedEx van pulled up in front of my house. The driver got out and was holding a small box.

"Oh, looks like that's for me. I'd better go," I said.

He nodded. "Okay, well I'll catch you later. I've got to get back to work anyway. I just stopped home to pick up a couple of things."

"Well, see you tomorrow, Jake."

"Count on it."

I walked back home, accepted the package, and opened it as soon as I stepped back inside. When I saw the contents, I gasped in shock.

A vibrator!

I took it out of the box and examined it, wondering what the big deal was. I knew my sister had once raved about hers, my mother had a collection of different sizes and speeds hidden somewhere under her bed, and Darcy – well she couldn't survive a night without one.

"Darcy, you little freak," I giggled, noticing that mine included the batteries and was ready to rock.

I looked at the clock and bit my lower lip. The kids wouldn't be home for another couple of hours.

Eh…what the hell.

***

Five minutes later, I lay in bed, trying to catch my breath. My legs were still trembling, my heart rate definitely up. I stared at the new toy and smiled.

Oh, my new friend. Where have you been all my life?

Chapter Fourteen

Later that night, I sat in the kitchen on my laptop and started searching the Internet for jobs in the area. When I came across an ad for a store clerk in a local boutique, I filled out an online application and sent it in. The pay wasn't the greatest, but it was definitely a start.

"Mom," said Regan, stepping into the kitchen holding out her cell phone. "It's grandma."

I sighed and grabbed the phone.

"Why haven't you been returning my calls?" murmured my mother. "You have no idea how worried I've been about you, dear."

I went over to my purse and pulled out my phone. She'd called twice in the last hour.

"Mom, you haven't given me a chance to call you back. Believe it or not, my phone isn't attached to my hip twenty-four hours a day," I said, sticking it into my back pocket.

"I keep mine with me all the time. You never know when there could be an emergency."

"Sorry, mom. Is it an emergency?" I asked rubbing my forehead.

"Apparently, it is. Regan told me that Scott is staying with his parents? What's going on?"

I paused, not sure how much to tell her. She'd be livid if she found out he'd been cheating on me. She'd probably be here in the morning when I awoke, packing up all of his things in garbage bags to be shipped out to the Goodwill.

"Well, we're having some problems and thought it would be better if we separated for a little while."

"Did he cheat on you?"

Why in the hell was that everyone's first guess?

"Mom, I don't really want to get into it."

"He did, didn't he? That selfish prick."

"Well, there's more to it than that," I said.

"Oh," she groaned, "don't let him off the hook; there are no excuses for cheating on your spouse."

I nodded. "I know, you're absolutely right, mom. Look, I have to go. I'll call you tomorrow and we'll talk about this."

"Lindsey, I'm flying out there," she said. "I'm not going to let you go through this all by yourself."

I groaned, inwardly. "Mom, it's okay, really. Darcy's been wonderful and we're all doing fine. You have your store to run and shouldn't abandon it."

"You're my daughter and much more important than any old store. Besides, Kyle can handle everything."

I started to pace. "Thanksgiving is coming up in two weeks. Why don't you just wait until then and fly out here? I'm really doing fine, mom. I swear."

She didn't say anything and I could picture the wheels turning in her head. Finally, she relented. "Okay. But if you need me, call me right away. I'll be out there faster than you can say 'Scott's a fucking idiot.'"

I laughed. "I will, mom. Otherwise, I'll see you on Thanksgiving."

"I love you, dear."

"I love you, too, mom."

I hung up the phone and handed it to Regan, who was eating a banana and watching me like a hawk.

"When *is* dad coming back home?" she asked.

I shrugged. "I really don't know, sweetheart."

She sighed and threw her banana peel away. "Well, I'm going to bed. I have a major test, tomorrow."

I walked over and kissed the top of her head. "Night."

I followed Regan upstairs and then stopped into Jeremy's room. He was on his computer and closed the window he'd been staring at when I walked inside.

"Hey, kiddo," I murmured, grabbing his dirty clothes hamper. "It's time to get ready for bed."

He sighed and then turned to face me. "Just a little longer?"

I looked at my watch. "It's nine o'clock."

He scowled. "Fine."

"Don't forget to brush your teeth before you fall asleep, too."

His last appointment with the dentist had been a major disappointment, three cavities and a referral for a nearby orthodontist.

"I know."

"Did you get all of your homework done?"

He snorted. "It was done *hours* ago."

I stared at him for a moment. "Are you okay?"

"Yeah, why wouldn't I be?"

"I just want to make sure. I know, with your father out of the house…"

"When is he coming back? He's been gone for almost two weeks."

I sat down on his bed. "I really don't know, honey. He might not."

His face darkened. "He wants to come back. It's your fault if he doesn't."

I sighed. "I know you can't possibly understand what's going on, and the less you know the better. Just remember we both love you and this has nothing to do with you."

"It's not fair. You won't tell us anything and expect it to be okay?"

"The only thing I can say is that it has to do with honesty and trust. If there isn't any in a relationship, then it won't last. Your father lied about a few things, very important things, and it's very difficult for me to let it go."

"Even though he loves all of us? What if he promised to never lie again, would you let him move back in?"

"Making promises and acting on them are not the same thing, Jeremy. Right now, I need time to think things over and he needs time to realize how very wrong he was, so that it doesn't happen again."

Just then my cell phone began to ring.

Darcy.

"Get your pajamas on," I said. "I'll be back soon to say goodnight."

"Fine," he mumbled.

"Hey, girlfriend," said Darcy, "how's it going?"

"Good," I cleared my throat. "I um…I received your little present today."

She chuckled. "Nice. Did you try it out yet?"

I paused, my face turning red at the memories of earlier.

"You did, didn't you?" she whispered. "Tell me I'm wrong but those things are better than chocolate!"

I laughed. "I wouldn't go that far…but they certainly have their uses."

She giggled wickedly. "So, did I do good?"

"It definitely brightened up my day."

"Good. Now, hate to change such a fun subject but I think I might have found you a job."

Thank God.

"Where?" I asked.

"The Sheriff's Department in Irondale. They're hiring for a *Records Keeper*."

I bit one of my nails. "Seriously?"

"Mm hmm…and I met Sheriff James earlier today, oh man talk about a freaking hunk! What is it with all these handsome devils in law enforcement?" she sighed. "Makes me want to commit a crime, just so I'll get frisked."

I laughed. "I know, right?"

"Anyway, he had some tax questions and that's why he'd stopped into the office. We got to talking and he said they needed someone right away since the other gal just up and left."

"How do I apply?"

She gave me the information and told me to send a resume.

I groaned. "One problem: I still don't *have* a resume."

"I kind of figured that. Don't worry, hon, I'll help you create one after work tomorrow night. Then, we'll email it directly to Sheriff James. From there, he can forward it to the Human Resources Department. Piece of cake."

I smiled. "Thanks, Darcy. You don't know how much all of this means to me."

She sighed. "You were there for me, sister. Just paying it forward."

"Well, thanks."

"I'd better go. Max just got out of bed."

"See you tomorrow," I answered.

"You too. Say hello to your little friend for me."

"Little friend?"

She chuckled.

"You're so bad," I whispered.

"I call mine 'Herbie' and when he goes bananas…good Lord, watch out!"

I laughed. "T.M.I. I'm ending this conversation right now."

She burst out laughing.

I hung up, put Jeremy to bed, then decided to do some reading. I grabbed the Kindle, went into my bedroom, and started searching for books that might help me figure things out with my husband. After finding one that interested me, I turned off my bedroom light and began reading. Within minutes, I drifted off.

Chapter Fifteen

I woke up in the middle of the night to a loud thump just outside of my bedroom window. Thinking it was a squirrel or the neighbor's pesky cat from across the road, I got out of bed, went to the window, and peeked through the blinds. Sure enough, the bush was moving, a sign that some sort of animal was probably lurking around in the yard.

Sighing, I closed the blinds and turned to get back into my bed when a pair of strong hands grabbed me and shoved me down onto the mattress. Before I could scream, the assailant covered my mouth with his gloved hand and straddled me between his thighs.

"Shut the fuck up," he growled, pushing against my mouth. "Don't give me a reason to kill you, bitch."

My eyes filled with tears as I stared up at the man whose face was covered by a black ski mask. All I could see were his glittery dark eyes and scowling mouth.

"I've got a message for you," he whispered, staring coldly into my eyes. Raising a switchblade, he pressed it against my cheek. "A warning. One that will allow you to live should you be intelligent enough to heed it. Keep your nose out of other people's business."

I stared into his cruel eyes, unable to breathe.

"Got that?" he asked, his breath hot on my face.

I nodded vehemently.

We stared at each other for what seemed like forever, when something changed in his expression. I recoiled in horror, recognizing the look.

"You smell good," he whispered huskily. He licked his lips and began moving a hand over my body, making me shudder in terror. I wasn't sure if he was going to rape me, kill me, or both. "If you tell anyone about his," he breathed, his hand squeezing my breast. "Anyone – you'll fucking die."

I closed my eyes and began crying into his glove.

He brushed his lips against my throat and then moved to my ear, breathing heavily. "You cause any trouble for anyone," he whispered, "your children will die first, and I'll make sure you get a front row seat."

My muffled cries turned to choked sobs and he squeezed my mouth painfully.

"Shut up," he spat, "or I'll kill everyone, right now. Wouldn't bother me in the least."

I reached somewhere inside and forced myself to quit sobbing for my children. They needed my courage more than anything at the moment.

"That's it," he whispered, loosening his grip on my mouth. After a few more horrifying minutes of being felt up, he lifted himself off of the bed and ran a finger down the sharp edge of the knife. "Just so you know," he smiled darkly, "I'll be watching you. You can't hide and don't even think about running. I have connections all over." Then he turned and slipped quietly out of my bedroom.

I didn't even hesitate; I immediately jumped out of bed and grabbed the metal bat hiding underneath it. Ironically, I'd hidden it there in case of intruders when Scott had begun "working" his longer hours. Breathing heavily, I moved slowly out of my bedroom and down the dark hallway towards the stairs, hearing nothing but the ticking of the Grandfather clock. When I heard a creak from somewhere upstairs, my heart stopped.

If that bastard touches my kids, I'll fucking kill him!

Fueled now by anger, I threw caution to the wind and rushed upstairs to their bedrooms, ready to fight to the death, if needed. When I found them both alone and safely sleeping, I whispered a silent prayer and then continued my search. When the rest of the house appeared empty, I sat down at the kitchen table and allowed myself to cry.

What do I do? What in the hell do I do?

I was so torn. The man had threatened to kill my children if I reported anything. I was certain that Jerry was responsible, so reporting the incident to the police wasn't even an option. I also considered calling Jake, but I knew he'd probably go after Jerry, which might provoke another visit from that monster. My gut told me he'd make good on his promise, too, if he returned.

I stood up and began to pace, trying to weigh my options. In the end, I decided to change the locks on all my doors and look into getting a gun.

Frightened and defeated, I stayed up the rest of the night, the bat on my lap and a butcher knife in my hand. When the morning sun began to rise, I put them both away and began making breakfast.

Chapter Sixteen

After the kids left for school, I took a shower with the bathroom door locked and the butcher knife next to my shampoo. I wasn't sure what my assailant was capable of, and remembering the way he'd felt me up, I wasn't about to let my guard down.

As I finished drying my hair, someone rang the doorbell. I stepped cautiously to my front door and peeked out the side window.

It was Jake.

I opened the door. "Hi."

"Morning," he said, staring down at my clothing, a loose tank top and jeans.

I cringed, suddenly remembering the morning jog he'd talked me into.

"You might want to change if you plan on joining me. Sweating in jeans isn't the most pleasant thing in the world." He was dressed in grey sweats and a dark blue T-shirt, looking ready to tackle the world.

I opened my mouth to respond, but nothing came out. It was an absolute struggle not to blurt out everything that had happened during the night, especially at that particular moment. He looked so confident and powerful, like he could handle anything thrown at him. But my children's lives were involved and I couldn't take any risks.

His eyes narrowed. "Lindsey, are you okay?"

I cleared my throat and produced a weak smile. "Yes, I'm fine."

He studied my face. "Did he show up last night?"

My heart skipped a beat. "What do you mean?"

"Did Scott give you trouble last night?"

I exhaled. "No, I haven't spoken to him since the other night, actually."

He frowned and rubbed his chin. "Are you sure you're okay?"

"I told you I'm fine. Why do you ask?"

"I don't know, you just seem… tense."

I shrugged. "I'm okay, just had a hard time sleeping last night."

He nodded. "So, I take it you're probably not energized enough for a run?"

"No, I'm sorry. I have a lot of errands to run today, ones that can't wait. What about tomorrow?"

"Okay. I guess I'll just have to suffer my own company this morning," he pouted.

Watching a hunk like him pout over me was almost enough to make me change my mind, but I wanted to switch my locks. I wouldn't feel even remotely safe until I did.

"I'm sorry," I said. "I promise I'll get more sleep tonight and join you in the morning. Same time?"

"Same time."

"Okay, well, I'll see you," I said, stepping backwards. As I was about to shut the door, he stuck his foot inside, blocking me from doing it. I opened it back up and gave him a puzzled look.

"You would tell me if anything was bothering you, right?"

His smile was disarming, and almost made me falter. "Sure," I answered, softly.

From the look in his eyes, I knew he wasn't really convinced. That wasn't good.

I stepped forward and touched his arm. "Jake, I just have so much going on in my life, with my husband and trying to find a job. It's exhausting, to say the least."

He stared at my hand and then our eyes locked. "Okay," he said. "Just remember, I'm here for you if you need someone to talk or a shoulder to lean on."

I nodded.

"Fuck it," he muttered, pulling me into his arms and holding me against his firm chest.

I released a sigh and closed my eyes. It felt good to be held by someone solid and so totally masculine. It even gave me a sense of security for the first time in days. Unfortunately, I also knew it was a false sense of security.

"Sorry," he murmured into my hair. "You just looked like you could use one of these."

"Actually, you were right," I whispered against his chest. "Thank you."

He tightened his arms around me. "You smell good," he said.

"So do you," I answered, catching a whiff of Irish Spring and toothpaste; he smelled like he'd just gotten out of the shower. An image of Jake with a towel around his waist and water dripping down his washboard stomach flashed through my head, and something in my own stomach went 'swoosh.'

"I suppose I should let you go. We don't want the neighbors gossiping," he teased.

I giggled nervously and stepped away from him. "Well, thanks."

"It's the least I can do. Although, I have to admit, it wasn't all for you," he said, his eyes burning into mine.

Before I could respond, he turned and left me standing on the porch, my mind buzzing with questions. I watched as he took off running down the street and wondered what the hell I was getting myself into now.

***

After I went to the hardware store and purchased new locks for the house, I decided to stop into a local gun shop I'd passed many times throughout the years. When I finally talked myself into getting out of my SUV and walking inside, I was not really prepared for the prices or how many types of guns there were to choose from. By the time I was approached by a salesperson, my head was spinning.

"First time in a gun shop?" asked the clerk, who didn't look old enough to handle a gun, let alone sell one.

I smiled. "Is it that obvious?"

He swept his hand over his floppy red hair and smiled. "Oh…just a little."

"Well, I am a little overwhelmed," I admitted.

"It's very understandable if you've never shopped for a gun before. What are your needs?

I raised my eyebrows.

What are my needs? Far too many to count.

"What I meant was, why do you want a gun?"

"Um, for protection."

"Okay. Have you ever shot a gun before?"

I shook my head. "I just want a handgun that's easy to use and doesn't cost a fortune."

He nodded and then began walking to one of the cases. "Let me show you one of our most popular revolvers. It's easy to load and unload, and the price is pretty reasonable."

"Okay, thank you."

He took out his keys and pulled out a small silver gun with a black handle. "This is a Taurus Ultra-Light Thirty-Eight Special. It's fast, reliable, and easy to carry."

It was also three hundred and fifty dollars. Luckily, I still had one credit card that wasn't maxed out.

I took the gun and held it. Even without bullets it felt so powerful in my hands. Powerful and a little scary.

He nodded towards the gun. "Before you fire that bad boy, we recommend you take some of our gun classes. We also have a shooting range in the back of our store, as well, for target practice."

I nodded. "Okay. So, you'll teach me how to shoot this thing?"

"Definitely. We can start right now with the basics."

Then, for the next ten minutes, he took me into the back and gave me a quick lesson on how to load and unload the gun, as well as what I'd need to do to actually clean it.

When he was finished, I took a deep breath. "Okay, I'll take it," I said.

"Well," he replied, grabbing a clipboard from underneath the counter, "fill out this form and when your background check is approved, you'll be able to purchase the gun."

I bit the side of my lip. "How long does it take?"

The young man shrugged. "A day or two. We'll call you when it's received."

Crap.

I had no choice but to wait. "Okay," I said, nodding. "Let's do it."

After I filled out the paperwork and left the store, my phone began to vibrate in my purse.

Scott.

Great, just what I needed.

"What is it?" I asked, getting into my SUV.

He chuckled. "Well, hello to you, too."

I closed my eyes and leaned back in my seat. "Sorry, I didn't sleep well last night."

He sighed. "I'm sure it's been difficult for you."

Do you think?

I almost went off on him but it was getting old. I was tired of arguing. "So, are you still at your parents'?"

"For now. I was hoping you'd let me come home."

I rolled my eyes. He was such a broken record.

"Don't start this again," I warned.

"Look, I know I made a mistake but I swear to you, it will never happen again."

"I…I just can't trust you," I said. "After everything that's happened. Plus, I'll never be able to get those images out of my head."

"We can go to counseling," he said. "I'll do whatever it takes to earn your trust back."

"Scott..."

"Please," he said, softly. "I miss you and the kids."

"I really need more time to think about this," I said. "Rushing me isn't going to help the situation."

He sighed. "Well, can I at least see our children?"

"Yes, of course."

"Friday night?"

"Sure. Why don't you pick them up after six?"

"I thought maybe we could all have dinner together?"

I groaned. "No, Scott. I need some space right now. Just, pick them up and spend time with them. They need you."

"Fine."

"I have to go," I said.

"Lindsey, no matter what happens, just remember, I love you and… I swear, I've never stopped."

You sure have an odd way of showing it.

"Goodbye, Scott," I mumbled, hanging up.

***

It was just after twelve when I arrived back home. The house appeared empty, but my nerves were on edge as I stepped through the door. Expecting the worst, I gripped my bat tightly and searched the house. Finding it empty, I grabbed a screwdriver from the garage and began changing all of the locks. As I was on my knees finishing up with the front door, Jake approached me. This time he was dressed casually in dark chinos and a white polo shirt.

"Good idea," he said, nodding towards the locks. "I was going to suggest that myself."

I stood up and smiled. "I suppose I should have done it right away."

"Well, you've had plenty of other things on your mind."

"Day off?" I asked, staring at his casual clothes.

"Yeah. I was thinking about grabbing a bite to eat. Have you had lunch yet?"

At the mention of food, I realized I was famished. I hadn't eaten anything since last night, and even that wasn't very much.

"I could eat," I said, hearing my stomach start to growl.

"How about joining me?"

"I don't know…"

"Come on, my treat again. You can buy next time."

I sighed. "Well, okay. I'd better change."

His caramel eyes swept over me, lingering a little longer than necessary on my chest. "You look great. Let's just go."

I looked down at my clothing – both the tank and jeans were beginning to hang in a very unflattering way since my appetite had basically disappeared in the last week. "Thanks, but I'm definitely not going anywhere with you in this. Just give me five minutes, please?"

He shrugged. "Okay, if it makes *you* feel more comfortable."

I opened the door and motioned him inside. "Come on in and wait. It's much cooler."

"Thanks."

He followed me in and I was suddenly very much aware of how incredibly sexy he was and how very alone we were.

I cleared my throat. "Uh, I'll be right back."

He sat down on the couch and spread his arms across the back. "Take your time."

I hurried to the bedroom and went through my closet. In the very back was a white and blue sundress I hadn't worn in a couple of years. Thankfully, it still looked new and wasn't too outdated. As I zipped up the back and studied myself in the mirror, I sighed with relief. The few pounds I'd shed in the last few days had allowed me to fit comfortably in the dress.

"Wow," smiled Jake as I stepped back into the living room, ten minutes later. I'd also applied a little makeup and managed to twist my hair into a chignon. "You look very lovely."

"Oh, well thank you," I said, brushing a loose strand of hair away from my eyes.

He stood up. "So, do you like seafood?"

I raised my eyebrows. "For lunch?"

His eyes glittered with amusement. "Why not?"

I broke into a grin. "Exactly, why not?"

An hour later we sat across from each other, sharing a large shrimp cocktail appetizer at "Benjamin's On the Lake."

"So," he asked. "Have any luck finding a job yet?"

"Not yet, although Darcy has a couple of leads for me; she's coming over tonight to help me with my resume."

He took a swig of his beer. "Sounds like Darcy is a very good friend."

I smiled. "She is. We've known each other for a long time. We've certainly been through a lot together."

"Is she married?"

I grinned. "Why? Are you interested?"

He shook his head. "No. I was just curious."

"She's going through a difficult divorce herself, but she's definitely available. Actually, she has expressed an interest in you, so if you change your mind –"

He chuckled. "No. I'm interested in someone else."

"Oh?" I asked, thinking of the cute brunette from the other day.

His eyes locked with mine. "Yeah but she has too much on her plate right now. However, I'm a patient guy and she's worth the wait."

My eyes widened. "Well, I uh…"

He put a hand over mine. "Shit, I didn't embarrass you, did I?"

The warmth of his hand on mine sent a heat wave all the way down to my toes. "No," I said. "You just shocked the hell out of me."

He squeezed my hand and released it. "Sorry. I just wanted you to know that I'm interested."

I stared at him, stunned. He was incredibly good-looking and could probably have anyone he wanted. "I don't know what to say. I guess I'm just kind of surprised."

He raised his eyebrows. "Why?"

"Well, you're attractive, single, and I'm sure you have women waiting in line to go out with you. I'm just a little confused as to why you'd be interested in me."

He leaned forward and his eyes burned into mine. "You really have no clue."

I chuckled as I raised my Bloody Mary to my lips. "No clue?"

"How bad I want you," he said, his eyes making a hot trail from my lips to my cleavage.

I choked and the spicy liquid burned all the way down my throat.

"You okay?" he asked, sitting up straighter as I hacked and sputtered all over my napkin.

I'm sorry…spicy drink," I replied hoarsely.

The gleam in his eyes told me he knew better. "Oh, I thought it was something else."

Feeling flushed, I fanned my face with my napkin. "Well, okay, maybe that too."

He leaned back and smiled. "Sorry. It's just that you had this look earlier today and it drove me crazy."

I raised my eyebrows. "What look?"

"This look" he said, rubbing his chin with an amused expression. "Like you were wondering..."

I raised my eyebrows. "Wondering what?"

His eyes darkened. "If you'd have the guts to sleep with me."

I felt an instant surge of hunger between my legs and wanted nothing more than to jump over the table, sit on his lap, and lick the beer from his moist lips with everything I had. But then I remembered I was still a married woman.

I snaked my hand away from his. "Jake…" I answered, my cheeks burning.

He let out a long breath. "Shit, I'm sorry. That was probably out of line."

I sighed. "Actually, I'm totally flattered. But…"

Jake took another swig of his beer. "I know. It's too soon. I totally understand that. It's just…"

"What?"

He took a deep breath. "Okay, I don't want to freak you out or embarrass you any further but…I just can't stop thinking about you. You're constantly on my mind, which is strange, because I know we've only just met."

I bit my lower lip. "You're constantly thinking about me?"

He smiled. "Yes, and dammit, you're making me lose sleep."

I blushed. "Sorry, I guess."

He reached over and brushed a strand of hair from my lips, his eyes burning into mine. "I just keep thinking about the way your eyes dance when you're laughing, or," he touched my lip, "how your teeth graze your lower lip when you're nervous. But mostly," he said, leaning back. "I look at you and everything you have to offer, and wonder how in the world Scott could have been such a fool."

"Well, thank you," I whispered, my stomach feeling all fluttery inside.

"You deserve to have someone who appreciates you. Who will be there for you through thick and thin, and never take you for granted."

I was so flattered that I didn't know what to say.

He sighed and went on. "Maybe it's because I've been through a similar situation and feel your pain, or finally know what I want in life, hell I don't know. What I do *know* is that I want to get to know you more, in every way."

"Um, okay," I breathed, feeling like a teenager on her first date.

He noticed my reaction and chuckled. "You're not going to avoid me now, are you? I know it's a lot to take in. If you want to run for the hills, I guess I wouldn't blame you."

I released a long breath and smiled. "No, actually, I'm glad you told me. It feels good to be wanted."

He smiled, wickedly. "Oh, you're definitely wanted."

Just then, the waitress came back with our food and we focused on the lobsters.

"Oh, this is so good," I said, dipping another piece of the succulent meat into the butter. "Thanks again for doing this."

He smiled. "You're welcome. I love a woman with a good appetite."

"No salad nibbler here," I said. "I have to have my meat and carbs."

"Couldn't agree more."

As I was taking a sip of water, I looked towards the bar where a man with a shaved head and a dark goatee sat staring at me. When he noticed me glancing back, he raised his drink and nodded. It brought back the threats from my intruder last night and all the blood rush to my ears.

"Oh, my God," I squeaked.

Jake leaned forward. "What's wrong? Are you okay?"

I glanced back at the stranger. He'd finished his drink and was preparing to leave.

"I…uh…"

Jake turned towards the bar as the man threw down some cash and strolled away casually.

Jake turned back at me and smiled. "What, was that guy leering at you?"

I looked at him but didn't know what to say.

"What is it?" he prodded. "You look like you just saw a ghost."

I shook my head. "It was nothing."

His eyes widened. "Nothing?"

Remembering the other man's threats against my children, I held my tongue. "I'm fine."

He stared at me for a few seconds and nodded. "Okay. Just remember, if you need to talk about anything, I'm here for you."

"Thanks," I answered.

His cell phone was resting on the table and it began to vibrate. He picked it up and listened to his message. "Shit. I swear I never get any rest."

"What is it?" I asked. "Do you have to stop into work, again?"

He stood up. "I hope not. I'm going to make a quick call. I'm sorry, I'll be right back."

"Of course."

When he walked away to use his phone privately, I tried to relax, although I was shaken from the stranger's attention. I also felt like everyone in the restaurant was staring at me and it took everything I had not to get up and leave.

"Close call," sighed Jake, sliding back into the booth, a few minutes later. "They were just looking for some paperwork that I must have forgotten to turn in."

"So, you're safe?"

"I'm safe," he grinned, "although, I'm not sure if you are, wearing that dress."

I shook my head and smiled.

"What?" he teased. "It's your fault. I'd planned on being a perfect gentleman until you walked out wearing that little number."

Just then *my* phone began to ring, startling us both. I took it out of my purse and frowned.

Scott.

I ignored the call and put it back into my purse.

"Not important?" he asked.

I shook my head. "No."

We finished our food and Jake asked for the bill when the waitress returned to check on us.

"What now?" he asked, putting his credit card away.

I smiled. "I should get back. The kids will be home in an hour or so."

He nodded. "I understand. Let's go."

It was stifling hot when we stepped out of the restaurant and I was slightly lightheaded from the cocktail. "Whoa," I breathed, stopping in my tracks. "I'm a little dizzy. That was one stiff drink."

He grabbed my hand and slid it around his bicep. "Here, hold on to me and I'll make sure you don't trip in those heels."

I smiled. "Okay."

Damn he felt good. His forearm was thick and hard and I imagined what he must look like when he was pumping iron, his muscles glistening with sweat, tightening and flexing, his face a hard mask of concentration. Possibly the same look he had when making love to a woman.

"You must work out," I blurted, before I could stop myself.

He looked down at me and smiled with amusement. "A little."

I stared at him in horror. "I'm sorry. That sounds like a stupid come-on or something. I can't believe I just said that."

He threw his head back and laughed.

"I mean seriously," I said, shaking my head. "You must think I'm this jilted, lonely housewife who's hitting on her hot neighbor. I feel like such a twit."

"So you think I'm hot?" he asked as we made it back to his car. He walked me over to the passenger side and opened the door.

I could feel my face burning brightly in the sun. "Well, I mean...you're very good-looking, obviously."

He stared into my eyes. "And you're...absolutely beautiful," he murmured.

The world around us seemed to have stopped as he moved towards me. Before I could catch my breath, he pulled me into his arms and crushed his lips against mine, surprising the hell out of me for the second time that afternoon. In that instant, something inside of me woke up and I abandoned all control, slipping my arms around his neck, pulling him in closer. As we melted together, his tongue moved into my mouth and I could taste mint along with a hint of Michelob.

Sensing my submission, he pushed me against the car and began exploring the inside of my mouth while I ran my fingers through his soft dark hair and held on. His tongue was hot, wet and demanding, like nothing I'd experienced in quite some time. I moaned into his mouth and pressed closer.

With a deep groan, his hands cupped my buttocks and began kneading my cheeks with his fingers, sending a fiery heat to my pelvis. When he pulled my hips in closer to his, I could feel his excitement, which was more than substantial.

"Jake," I breathed, as his mouth moved lower.

He cupped one of my breasts and began kneading it. "Fuck, I want you, right now," he growled into the curve of my neck.

And I wanted him.

Badly.

Hearing laughter in the distance, however, I remembered where we were and opened my eyes. Thankfully, we were parked on the side of the building and had some privacy, but not enough for what either of us really wanted.

"Jake," I repeated, pushing him back. "This…"

He stiffened up and closed his eyes. "I know. What the hell am I even thinking? I'm sorry."

I shook my head. "No, it's okay. Obviously, I enjoyed it as much as you did."

He opened his eyes and they burned into mine. "I want this to go further, more than anything," he said. "But, only when you're ready."

As far as my body went, I was beyond ready. I wanted someone to drive me crazy with everything he had, make love to me like I was the only woman he'd ever wanted. Take me to places that I hadn't seen in years. But I knew in my heart, at that particular moment, it wasn't right. Not right now and not with someone who was almost a stranger.

I let out a breath. "I guess I know what I want sexually, but I'm not ready for it emotionally. I'm sorry."

"Well, I'm willing to wait. Besides, if you were easy, I wouldn't even be interested. I can get that anytime I want," he said as I slid into the car.

"I'll bet," I breathed, staring at him as he walked back around to the driver's side.

"Now," he said, getting inside. "Let's get home so I can take a cold shower and forget about the way your sweet ass felt in the palm of my hands."

I shook my head and smiled.

Chapter Seventeen

Neither of us said much on the way home, we just listened to one of his old Eagles CDs in a comfortable silence; every once in a while, however, I'd catch him stealing a glance towards me or smiling to himself. It wasn't until we pulled onto our street that reality set back in.

"Shit," said Jake, as he pulled into his driveway. "Looks like you've got company."

Scott's car was in the driveway and he was sitting on my porch, looking less than pleased.

"Would you like me to come over?" asked Jake. "He looks a little pissed off."

I sighed. "I don't think it's a good idea," I said. "But thanks."

"Are you sure?"

I nodded. "I'll be fine. Thanks for lunch, by the way."

"You're welcome."

Afraid that he was going to try and kiss me, I got out of the car and walked home as casually as I could, under the circumstances.

"My…my…my," sneered Scott as I stepped up and onto the porch. "Looks like you're moving on with your life. New locks on the house, new boyfriend…"

"He's not my boyfriend," I interrupted. "I'm married, remember? Oh, that's right – you're the one who forgets that little fact the moment he steps into his office. Don't you dare start pointing fingers at me, Scott. You definitely won't win that argument."

He blew out a long breath and nodded. "Yeah, you're right. I'm being a total shit. *You* certainly don't deserve getting the third degree."

I sighed. "Thank you. Now, what do you want?"

"Is that a new outfit," he asked, staring at my clothes.

I raised my chin. "No, I've had this forever. Why are you here?"

He ran a hand over his face and I noticed for the first time, how haggard he looked. "Isn't it obvious?" he asked. "I just want to come home."

"It's been less than two weeks. I'm not ready to let you back home."

He gave me an incredulous look. "Why?"

"Are you daft? How many times do we have to go over this? *Because*, I can't get those images out of my head and, to be frank, I don't know if I can really ever trust you again."

He ran a hand through his blonde hair. "Fuck, Lindsey, I swear to you, it will never happen again."

"It shouldn't have happened to begin with," I said.

He nodded and looked away. "I know."

"Please, give me time to think. I really need it, Scott. You owe me that much."

His head bobbed up and down. "Yeah, you're right," he said, standing up.

"You're still taking the kids Friday, right?"

He put his hands on his hips. "Personally, I still think we should do something as a family."

"No. You need to spend some quality time with the children."

"Have you told them anything about what happened?"

"I told them we needed some time away from each other."

"So, you didn't tell them what actually happened."

I looked at him in horror. "Are you kidding? They'd never look at you the same way again."

He smiled, bitterly. "Well, thanks for that."

I sighed. "Did you need some more clothes?"

"As a matter of fact, I do."

I unlocked the door and he followed me into our bedroom. When I bent down to pull out the suitcase from under the bed, he did the same and we bumped heads together.

"Oh...I'm sorry," I said, laughing. "Are you okay?"

"I'm fine," he said, looking at my forehead. "You have a little red mark, though."

I touched my head and winced. "It only hurts when I laugh."

He burst out laughing and then stared into my eyes. "I love you," he stated, trying to pull me into his arms. "Please, let me just hold you for a minute."

"Scott," I said, pushing him away. "Please...don't."

He grabbed the back of my head and pulled me to his lips, then began kissing me. I started pushing him away but then the ache in my heart cried out for my husband, who I knew I still loved regardless. His touch and taste were as familiar as the memories we'd shared.

Perhaps we *could* work it out?

I sighed and gave in, letting him kiss me.

He pushed me down against the bed and began touching my breasts. "Oh, baby, I want you so bad," he whispered.

I closed my eyes as he began fumbling around, trying to get under my dress. Unfortunately, as the seconds ticked by, I started thinking about those same hands on the other women and the look of bliss on his face when I'd found him getting a blowjob. I suddenly felt sick to my stomach as he unzipped his pants and his erection brushed against my thigh.

"Scott," I said, stiffening up.

"Are you ready for me?" he whispered as his intrusive hands slipped inside of my panties.

I sighed. "Stop."

"Feel this," he whispered, putting my hand on his crotch. "I still want you, baby." This time I shoved him back so roughly that he stared at me in shock. "Linds?"

"I can't do this," I mumbled, as he tried grabbing my hand again.

"But I love you, honey," he pleaded, his eyes filling with frustrated tears. "Please, we can work this out."

"Maybe someday," I said, getting off the bed. "But not right now."

"Come on, Lindsey," he begged, holding his hand out towards me. "Don't be like this."

"Listen, the kids will be home soon. Grab what you need and leave." Then I left the bedroom before he could say anything more and went to the kitchen. Fortunately, he didn't follow me and I had time to collect myself.

"Hi, mom," said Regan when she walked in the door ten minutes later. "Is dad home?"

Before I could answer, Jeremy raced through the door, a large smile on his face. "Dad's home?!"

I sighed. "He's…"

"Hey, kids!" hollered Scott, coming into the kitchen.

"Daddy!" cried Regan as she flew into his arms.

He picked her up and spun her around. "I've missed you, princess."

"Is she finally letting you back home?" asked Jeremy, scowling at me.

Scott put Regan down and stepped over to Jeremy. "Hey, don't blame your mother. This isn't her fault."

His eyes narrowed. "Do you want to come home?" he asked.

Scott put a hand on his shoulder. "Son, of course I do."

Jeremy turned to me. "Do you want dad to come home?"

I sighed. "Jeremy, it's complicated."

His face darkened as he looked back at his father. "It's her, isn't it? She won't let you back in because she's having an affair."

"Jeremy!" I snapped. "I am not having an affair!"

"Don't lie," he said, tears forming in his eyes. "First you kick dad out, then you go and have your hair done, now a new dress?"

"She is not having an affair," said Scott, although the look in his eyes told me he wasn't so sure about it, either.

"Honey," I said. "I would never do that to your father."

"Well, then, why can't you just move back home?" he asked Scott.

Scott let out a long sigh. "Well, it's not that easy. I'm going to level with you, because you deserve to know and I don't want you blaming your mother."

I raised my eyebrows.

"I lied to your mom about some things and deceived her. I hurt her very badly and she needs time to heal," he said, looking at me. "But, that doesn't mean we don't love each other."

"But…" whined Jeremy.

"No *but*s, Jeremy," replied Scott sternly. "I was a complete jerk and deserve to this and probably more. So, don't you dare go blaming your mother; she did absolutely nothing wrong."

Jeremy looked at me and sighed.

I wanted to forgive Scott more than anything at that moment, but I still wasn't sure if I could. I knew if we did get back together, it would probably be after many hours of therapy.

"So," said Scott, clapping his hands. "This Friday night, I'm taking you two and we're going out on the town and then we'll stay at grandma and grandpa's. Sound like fun?"

Both kids appeared elated at that announcement and I was able to let out a sigh of relief.

Scott looked at his watch and frowned. "Oh, I have a meeting I really need to get to. I'd better run. I'll pick you guys up at seven o'clock on Friday."

I wondered if his meeting included the two bimbos from the other day. I pushed the jealous thoughts aside, however, and forced a smile.

"I'll see you Friday, Linds," he said, kissing my cheek.

"Okay," I said, stiffening up as he pulled me in closer for a tight hug.

"Call me if you need anything," he whispered into my ear. "And I mean anything. I still have a hard on with your name on it."

That would have delighted me two weeks ago. Now, it only troubled me. I gently pushed him away and gave him a look that said, "Not funny."

He shrugged and then said his goodbyes to the children.

"I wonder where he's taking us?" asked Regan after Scott had left.

"Probably, to a nice restaurant," I said, handing her an apple.

Just then the telephone rang.

"It's Darcy," said Regan, looking at the caller I.D.

I grabbed the phone. "Hey, chic."

"You still up for working on your resume tonight?" she asked.

"Of course."

"Good, I'll be over in an hour. I'm dropping Max off at his father's then I'll swing by."

"See you soon, Darce."

"Darcy's coming over?" asked Jeremy.

I nodded. "Yes, she's going to help me find a job."

"You have a job," he said. "Taking care of us."

I smiled. "Even though I love that job, I need a second one that pays the bills."

He frowned. "So that means dad's not coming home soon."

"I don't know. I think that even if he does, it might be a good idea for me to earn some extra money anyway. Don't you think?"

He shrugged. "I don't know. I'm going on my computer for a while."

"Do you have homework?" I asked.

"Did it at school."

"Good job."

He left and I looked at Regan, who was staring at my outfit. "Where did you get that outfit, mom?"

"I found it in my closet. I lost a couple of pounds and it finally fit."

"It doesn't fit that well around your chest," she said.

I sighed. "I know."

"But you still look nice," she said.

I smiled. "Thanks, honey."

She left the kitchen and I started unloading the dishwasher. After adding the dirty dishes, my cell phone began to ring. The phone number appeared as a private one.

"Hello?" I asked.

"Stay away from the cop," whispered a feminine voice.

"Excuse me?"

I heard a choked sob and then the woman hung up.

Staring at my phone, I felt a cold shiver go down my spine.

Chapter Eighteen

Darcy breezed through my front door shortly after six, carrying two iced coffees and an excited gleam in her eye. The look on her face made me forget about the strange call, which I'd come to the conclusion had been Tina trying to warn me about her husband.

"Spill the beans," I said. "What's with the pleased look on your face?"

She took a sip of her coffee and smiled. "I have a date Saturday night."

I raised my eyebrows. "With who?"

"This guy I met on the Internet."

I frowned. "What do you mean? Where?"

She waved her hand. "Oh, just on one of those online dating services. Anyway, we're going out to dinner and then…well, who knows."

The look on her face told me that after dinner, she planned on making him the dessert.

"Do you know anything about your date?" I asked.

"Well, I know he's some kind of investor and travels a lot. He looks pretty handsome in his picture and has never been married, so no extra baggage. Unlike me."

"How old is he?"

She shrugged. "Around our age."

I sighed. "Well, just be careful. It makes me a little nervous that you're meeting up with someone from the Internet you've never met before."

"Hey, it's a lot safer than meeting a man when I'm already inebriated at the local bar. Anyway, everyone's doing it these days."

I pointed to her. "Well, you'd better call me as soon as you're done with him."

"He may never leave," she said with a wicked grin.

"Then call me between orgasms," I said.

She licked her lips and smiled. "My mouth might be full."

"You are so bad!"

"Speaking of being bad, maybe I can get him to spank me, too," she said with a wistful look.

I rolled my eyes. "Oh, for the love of God…"

"Hey, sister, don't knock it until you've tried it."

I raised a hand and laughed. "No thanks, I'll just take your word for it."

She grinned. "Wimp."

"I won't argue that."

She shook her head and glanced at her watch. "Okay, we should probably get started on that resume."

I led her to my computer and we spent the next hour trying to glamorize my short career as a fast food cashier, back when I was in my teens.

"Well, at least you have some current experience on the computer and are a pretty fast typist. Those online classes have to count for something, as well. Anyway, I'll send this off to Sheriff James and see if they're still hiring."

"Thanks, Darcy."

"No problem. It gives me a chance to correspond with the hunky sheriff a little more, too."

I laughed. "Oh, the stud-muffin sheriff; I should have known why you were so gung-ho on helping me get a job at that place."

She wiggled her eyebrows. "Girl, if you saw him, you'd understand."

"That's what you always say."

"No, *this* time I'm serious."

"Right."

She laughed.

"Tell you what, if I get a job with the sheriff, I'll tell him what an awesome woman you are and then find a way to set you two up."

"In that case, I better send him your resume tonight!"

I winked at her. "That's what I'm thinking."

"So, do we have everything?" she asked, scanning over my resume again.

I sighed. "It is. Kind of pathetic, huh?"

She shook her head. "No, not at all. You spent most of your adult life taking care of your kids. That's a lot of work and it's admirable. Don't be ashamed of it."

I smiled. "Thanks. I still wish I would have taken a part-time job or something. Every time I brought it up, however, Scott put the kibosh on it."

"Well, now you're on your own and can make those decisions all by yourself. Freedom is a very empowering."

"I wish I could feel it. Right now I feel trapped more than anything."

"It will get better. Take it from me."

I nodded.

"Okay," she said, looking at her watch. "Well, I'd better get going. I need to do some laundry when I get home."

I walked her to the door and gave her a big hug. "Thanks again, chick. I don't know what I'd do without you."

"That goes both ways," she said. "Listen, I'll talk to you either tomorrow or Friday. I still plan on taking you shopping before my date, Saturday as well. We'll go to the mall; I want to purchase something sexy to wear."

"Okay, thanks," I said, opening the door to let her out.

"Yumalicious," said Darcy, staring outside.

I peered around her and noticed Jake coming towards us in the darkness.

"Hi there," I said as he stepped up to the porch.

"Hi, ladies. I was just stopping by on my way to work to find out how you were doing, Lindsey."

I smiled. "Well, thank you. I'm doing fine."

Darcy held out her hand. "I don't think we've been formally introduced, I'm Darcy."

He took her hand and gave her one of his sexy smiles. "I'm Jake Sharp, nice to meet you."

"So Lindsey tells me you're in law enforcement? How exciting," she purred.

"Well, it definitely has its moments," he answered, looking amused.

"I bet," she said.

"Looks like you dropped something, Lindsey," he said, bending down to pick up the screwdriver I'd forgotten on the porch.

Darcy and I both stared at his firm behind. She quickly turned to me and nodded her approval.

Stifling a giggle, I gave her a warning look as he turned back around to face us.

"Well," said Darcy, clearing her throat. "Although, I'd love to stay and chat, I really have a lot of things to do tonight. It was very nice meeting you, Mr. Sharp."

"Just call me Jake."

Her eyes gave him the once-over. "No, I think 'Sharp' is much more appropriate."

Jake's eyes met mine and he smiled.

I could only groan.

She burst out laughing. "Sorry, Jake. I live for embarrassing my little friend here," she said, hip-checking me.

"Thanks."

"Talk to you tomorrow, Linds," she said, stepping off the porch.

"Okay," I said.

After she left, Jake folded his arms across his chest and studied me. "So, what happened with Scott?"

I sighed. "He's still trying to come back home."

He nodded. "I figured as much. I guess I don't really blame him."

"Well…"

"Do *you* want him to come back home?" he asked.

I stared at him, and right then and there, the answer rolled easily off my tongue. "No, I guess I don't."

He grinned. "Good. Because I don't like to share."

My cheeks turned pink as I thought about earlier. We'd both acted like a couple of horny teenagers, and now that my head had cleared, I felt silly. "Jake…"

He moved towards me and slipped his arms around my waist. "Shh…it's okay," he murmured, nuzzling my neck. "Let me just breathe you in for a second before I go to the stakeout."

I pushed him away and looked up into his eyes. "Stakeout? That sounds dangerous."

He smiled seductively. "You're already starting to worry about me? I like that, it turns me on."

I rolled my eyes. "Just be careful."

"I will – if you give me a goodnight kiss," he prodded.

I glanced across the street at the homes facing us, already feeling like the other neighbors had their noses pressed against their windows, gawking at us. "I can't," I whispered. "The kids might come out here, and they wouldn't understand."

He pulled me into the corner of the porch where the shadows surrounded us. "I think you can," he said, caressing my buttocks with the palms of his hands, sending a rush of heat to my pelvis. "Just one little kiss for luck, tonight?"

I could see the fire burning in his sultry eyes and couldn't resist. "For luck," I whispered right before his mouth captured mine, taking my breath away. I closed my eyes as one of his hands moved up and slid into my hair, holding me in place while the other pulled my hips against his. When I felt his hardness pressing against my stomach, it took everything I had not to reach for it.

"Jake," I breathed, pushing him away. "We really have to stop doing this."

"Why?" he whispered, staring at my lips. "We're both adults."

Just then, a white car pulled to a stop right in front of my house.

"Anyone you know?" Jake asked me as we stepped out of the shadows.

I shook my head. "No."

We watched as the person let the car idle while he lit a cigarette. I could see the clear silhouette of a bald head as the lighter flickered out and the hair stood up on the back of my neck.

The guy from the restaurant?

"Well," said Jake when the man eventually pulled away. "I supposed I'd better go. Hey," he said, staring down at me with concern. "Are you okay?"

I stared at him for a minute, wanting so much to tell him what had happened the night before, but the stranger's warnings wouldn't allow me to. I'd never risk the lives of my children.

"I'm fine. Just tired," I said.

He smiled. "Well, get a good night's sleep. If you feel like running tomorrow, I'll be stretching out at ten o'clock sharp."

I nodded. "Okay."

He moved towards me again as if he was going to kiss me, when the front door opened.

"Hey, Jake," said Jeremy, stepping onto the porch. "I thought it was just Darcy and mom out here."

"Darcy just left," said Jake. "By the way, is your computer running any better?" he asked.

Jeremy nodded vehemently. "Yeah, thanks for cleaning it up. It runs so much faster now. It's like night and day."

"Good, now remember what I told you and be very careful of what you're downloading on the Internet," said Jake with a stern look. "Some websites are a haven for viruses which will destroy your computer. Stay away from those sites and you won't have to worry about your computer acting up again."

I raised my eyebrows. Jeremy's face was flaming red and he looked slightly mortified. I began to wonder which websites he was referring to.

"It wasn't me," stammered Jeremy. "It was Hugo."

"What kind of websites are we talking about?" I asked.

Jake smiled. "Just some stupid sites hosting malware that the boys must have clicked on by accident. No big deal, I helped him fix it the other day after his computer froze up."

"Thanks," I said. "We can't afford to buy him a new computer, obviously."

"His should work just fine now. Well, I'd better get going. Jeremy, take care of your mother and your computer," said Jake, walking down the stairs. "Okay, bud?"

"Yeah, sure," said Jeremy. "See you, Jake!"

Jake waved and then jogged back to his house.

"That guy is cool," said Jeremy. "He knows a lot about computers."

"Lucky for you. Now, let's go inside."

It was after nine by the time I'd gotten both kids showered and ready for bed. I then double-checked to make sure all of the new locks were engaged, grabbed the butcher knife from my kitchen, and filled up the tub in the bathroom. It had been a long day and I wanted to end it early by trying to relax in a warm bubble bath as if everything was normal. Needless to say, clearing my mind of the last twenty-four hours was next to impossible. As I closed my eyes and tried to let go, all I could think about was the man who'd broken into my home and threatened my children, and the other man, who'd lived in my home and threatened our marriage.

My life was beginning to resemble a *Lifetime* movie.

Chapter Nineteen

It was my landline phone that woke me up early the next morning. When I saw who was on the other end calling me at such an absurd hour, I groaned.

"Hi, mom," I said, resting the phone on my shoulder.

"Hello, sweetheart."

I looked at the clock. "It's only six o'clock here, even earlier for you, why are you up so early?"

"I just couldn't sleep," she said. "I kept worrying about you and decided to call."

"I'm fine. How about we talk when the sun is up?"

And I've had enough coffee to tackle you.

She ignored me and cleared her throat. "Lindsey, I've been thinking, you and the kids should move out here with me. I have plenty of room and I can even offer you a job at the store."

"Oh, mom, that's a great offer but the kids would be livid if I took them out of their comfort zone. All of their friends are here and Scott would never agree to that."

"Who gives a shit about that bastard?" she said, in a thick voice.

I raised my eyebrows. "Mom, have you been drinking?"

"Oh, I may have had a couple of drinks," she said. "But this is about you, not me."

I sighed. "Are you okay?"

She paused for a few seconds.

"Mom?" I prodded. "Talk to me."

"It's Kyle," she said. "We're…we're not together anymore."

I sat up. "No! What happened? You must be going crazy."

"I'm fine. Actually, I asked him to leave, honey."

"Seriously?" I asked, trying to hide the relief in my voice. Kyle had always annoyed me. He wasn't much older than I was, but his attitude was always slightly condescending, as if his intellect was far more superior to mine.

"Oh, he was getting a little too controlling. Kind of like your husband, if you really want to know the truth."

I raised my eyebrows. "You thought Scott was controlling, too, huh?" I asked.

She snorted. "Is a tomato a fruit?"

I giggled. "I'm still up in the air about that one."

"Anyway," she said. "Now that you've kicked out Scott, I started thinking about Kyle and you know what? I was actually a little jealous that you were free and I had a deadbeat living with me. One who was trying to manipulate everything in my life but not contributing anything but sex."

I cringed. "Oh, mom…"

She chuckled. "He certainly had the tools and knew how to use them. But a stiff wanker doesn't pay the bills, you know, my dear?"

I shuddered, trying not to imagine Kyle and my mom in the wild throes of passion.

"Anyway," she sighed, her voice tinged with melancholy. "He's gone."

I sighed. "Well, you still don't sound very happy."

She cleared her throat. "It's still hard, letting someone go."

I nodded. "I know that all-too well."

"Yes, unfortunately you do."

"Well, so what are you going to do about the shop?"

"Aunt Ruthie is going to be helping me run it until I hire a new assistant fulltime. You know, that would be the perfect position for you, honey."

I bit the side of my lip. "Well, I don't know. I'd have to really think about it."

"The kids could just as easily make friends out here."

I rubbed my forehead and nodded. "I suppose."

The truth of the matter was, I didn't know if I could leave Darcy. She'd already done so much for me and we were so damn close.

"Well, I'd better call Ruthie and let her know that I'm not coming in this morning. We'll talk more about this when I get into town for the holidays."

"Okay, mom."

"Love you, honey."

"I love you, too."

After I hung up with her, I went to the kitchen and made a cup of coffee. As I waited for it to fill, I thought about my mother's offer and decided that it would never really work. Although I loved her dearly, I wasn't about to relive the days of being bossed around by her, even if I was getting paid for it. It was a nice gesture, but not in the best interests of my sanity.

Satisfied with my decision, I added cream to my coffee and then went over to the kitchen table where my cell phone was resting. After noticing that my message light was blinking, I picked it up and read the screen.

Stay away from the cop!

The message had come late in the night from an unknown number.

Frowning, I sent a message back.

Who is this?

After waiting ten minutes, I received another text.

Who is this? They asked.

I sighed and answered back. *You sent me a text late last night. Who are you?*

I watched my phone but the other person didn't respond. Then a horrible thought flashed through my brain. What if Tina had sent me the message secretly last night and now her husband had received my response this morning? Had I just set Tina up with another beating from her maniacal husband?

I began to panic, wondering what I should do. I very well couldn't go over there to check on her, I was much too terrified and didn't want my children hurt. Not for her or anyone else.

Then it hit me.

We *could* stay with my mother, if only temporary. My kids would be much safer out there and I wouldn't have to worry about feeling threatened anymore. I could also let Jake know what was happening and he could help me without the risk of harm to my kids.

I quickly called my mother back.

"You've reconsidered?" she squealed, still much more excited than I was.

"Well, actually I want it to be a temporary thing," I said. "I'd like to bring the kids out for a couple of weeks, maybe longer. Nothing permanent."

"What about school?" she asked.

"I haven't really figured that out yet," I said. "I'm sure I could work something out with their teachers. Like I said, it would only be temporary, until I've taken care of some problems out here."

"Well, let me know when you're coming out," she yawned.

"I will. I'm still going to have to discuss it with Scott and the kids, but I'll call you when I figure things out."

"Okay."

After I hung up the phone, I decided to dangle the idea in front of the kids during breakfast. Their reactions were better than I expected.

"Are you serious!" cried Regan. "A trip to Florida! That would be totally awesome!"

"Just for a couple of weeks," I said, hoping it wouldn't be any longer. "Grandma is lonely and needs company. She broke up with Kyle."

"He was a loser," said Jeremy. "I'm glad she kicked him to the curb."

I bit back a smile. "Wow, don't hold back. Tell me more."

"I can't. You'd ground me for using such inflammatory language."

I ruffled his hair. "Well, then, thanks for sparing our ears."

"You're welcome," he said.

"Anyway, we have to talk to dad about this first," I said, grabbing the syrup from the refrigerator.

Jeremy's face lit up. "Does this mean you're staying back here with dad, to try and work things out?"

"I'm staying behind because I need to find a job," I said, handing him his plate of pancakes.

"Well, I'm all for it," he said, spreading butter over his food. "I need a change. It's been too stressful around here."

"I know," I said. "And I'm really sorry about that."

He shrugged.

"Well, what about school?" asked Regan.

"That's what I'm going to have to figure out," I said. "It's almost Thanksgiving and you'll have some time off anyway. I'm hoping it won't interfere with your grades too much, and that they can give you homework to do while you're out there."

"I wonder what dad will say," said Jeremy, between bites.

"Oh, I'm sure he'll be fine with it. Besides, it's only for a couple of weeks," I said.

"I can't wait to go," said Regan with a wistful look. "We can hang out at the beach and go to Disneyworld. Oh, my God," her eyes widened. "You *have* to take me shopping! I need some new clothes."

"We'll need to talk to dad about that, too," I said, knowing it would be his wallet paying for everything.

After the kids left for school, I called Scott's cell phone and left him message to call me back. Then I vacuumed the floors and did some laundry. As I was folding towels, I received a phone call from the gun shop. They'd already received the approval for my license.

"I'll be over soon," I said, more determined than ever to purchase my handgun.

"We're open until eight o'clock tonight," the man said.

I hung up and took a shower. As I finished getting dressed, my doorbell rang.

"I'm beginning to think you're avoiding our morning jog," said Jake, eyeing my jeans and light blue peasant top.

"Oh, crap. I totally forgot." I said, looking down at his hand, which was freshly bandaged. "Hey, what happened there?"

He raised his fist and smiled. "I just got into a little scuffle last night. No big deal."

My eyebrows shot up. "A scuffle? Are you okay?"

"I'm fine."

I sighed. "Well, I guess my kiss didn't help you very much."

He stared at my lips. "Sure it did. I'm not dead."

I laughed. "Well, I guess that's one way to look at it."

"You know what?" he asked, licking his lips.

"What?'

With a determined look on his face, he moved towards me, kicked the door closed with the back of his shoe, and grabbed me around waist. "Maybe we should try for more than a kiss this time."

"Jake," I squealed, as his good hand slid over my butt and squeezed it tightly.

"Like I said before," he said, "sex is a great way to bring the heart rate up. But, to tell you the truth, you bring mine up every time I'm near you."

"We can't," I whispered.

"Okay," he said, sliding a hand over my blouse. "Then how about a little motivation, to get me going since you're obviously not coming with me once again?"

"To get you going?" I could tell from the swelling in his shorts, he *was* ready to go.

"Jesus, you feel so good," he groaned, squeezing my right breast. "I couldn't stop thinking about you all night. The things I wanted to do to you…"

I closed my eyes as his fingers sought my nipple through the fabric and I felt my sex contract. Before I knew what was happening, he'd lifted both my shirt and peach lace bra, exposing my bare skin.

"Jake," I moaned as his tongue replaced his fingers, sending hot tingles all the way down to my pelvis.

"Lindsey, you're so beautiful," he whispered, flicking the tip of my nipple.

I was completely on fire as his warm mouth moved to ravage my other one. I grabbed the back of his head and held on as he became more demanding with my breasts, squeezing, licking and nibbling. If it hadn't been for the sudden shrill ringing of my phone, I would have given him anything he wanted, right there in the entryway.

"Ignore it," he growled.

"I can't. It could be the school."

"Fuck," he groaned as I pushed him away to answer the phone.

I cleared my throat. "Hello?"

"Lindsey?" said the voice on the other end.

Crap, my mother-in-law.

"Hi, Molly."

She sighed. "Have you seen Scott?"

"He was here for a little while, yesterday evening. Why?"

She sighed. "Because he didn't come home last night."

I sighed. "Well, he's made some new friends. I'm sure he'll turn up."

"I've left several messages for him. It's not like Scott to ignore my calls."

Maybe he's too busy screwing his co-workers to answer mommy's call.

"Well, I'll try calling him again later. If I talk to Scott, I'll let him know you're worried, Molly."

"Thanks, Lindsey," she let out a ragged sigh. "I'm sorry about everything. He didn't get into specifics, but I know he hurt you."

"It's not your fault, but thanks."

"He adores you, you know."

"He has a funny way of showing it," I answered, dryly.

"Oh, everyone makes mistakes, Lindsey. Why, his father and I have had our problems throughout the years, but we've always managed to pull through. I know you and Scott will, too."

"Maybe. Listen, I've got to go. Scott's picking up the kids tomorrow night. I'm sure I'll talk to him before then and I'll have him call you."

"Okay, thank you."

After I hung up with her, I turned around to face Jake, who was regarding me curiously.

"I should really get going," I said. "My errands."

"What was that all about?" he asked.

"What, the phone call?"

He nodded. "Yeah. Something about Scott?"

I shrugged. "I guess he didn't show up at his parents' home, last night and now his mother's worried."

He snorted. "What is he, ten?"

I laughed. "I know. They've always coddled him."

"Where do you think he is?"

"Considering his mood when he left here, more than likely, he's with one of his new girlfriends."

His eyebrows shot up. "What kind of mood was that?"

"The same kind you were in a few minutes ago," I teased.

His face darkened. "Did he try anything with you?"

It was a bizarre conversation – my "almost" lover asking if my husband had tried anything with me.

"Nothing happened, although he certainly wanted it to."

He swore under his breath. "I shouldn't have left you alone with him."

I walked over to Jake and put a hand on his forearm. "He's not dangerous and I can certainly handle myself. He's just having a hard time with all of this."

His nostrils flared. "Having a hard time is what put him in this position to begin with. As far as I'm concerned, he doesn't deserve to be anywhere near you, let alone try to fuck you."

His harsh words startled me. "He's still the father of my children, Jake. I have to see him, like it or not."

He stared at me for a few seconds and then his expression softened. "I'm sorry. It just burns me that your husband took you for granted the way he did."

"I'm not going back to him," I stated. "I've made up my mind."

A wicked smile curled on one side of his mouth. "I know that. Not while I'm around."

I tilted my head and smiled back. "You're pretty confident of yourself, Detective Sharp, aren't you?"

Jake pulled me close and stared down into my eyes. "I'm sure that you deserve better and I 'm willing to give it to you, if you let me."

"Somehow, I believe that you will."

He started kissing me again, his hands wandering to my backside.

"Stop," I laughed, pushing him away. "I have things to do and you were on your way down the street, if I remember correctly."

He adjusted his shorts and smiled. "How am I supposed to run with a hard-on?"

Although, I seriously wanted to help him get rid of it, I just couldn't take that next step. Not yet. "You live right next door, go home and take a cold shower."

His eyes darkened. "How about a hot shower? There's room in there for two."

"Enough! God, you don't give up easily, do you?"

Sighing, he moved towards the door. "Not when I know what's involved."

"I'll talk to you later," I said.

He turned to me and smiled. "Oh, we'll be doing more than talking."

I grabbed the pillow from my loveseat to throw at him but he ducked out of the door laughing before I had a chance to hit him.

"Men," I grunted, although I couldn't wipe the smile from my face as I watched him jog back towards his house, one hand hiding his crotch.

Chapter Twenty

Two hours later, I walked out of the gun store with my new Taurus, along with ammunition and a gun case. One of the clerks, a heavyset guy with tattoos all over his arms and plates in his ears, had given me a quick lesson on firing at their shooting range, which was behind the store. Although, I probably couldn't hit anything yet, I now had a general idea on how to load the gun and fire it, if needed.

I hid the gun up in my bedroom closet as soon as I arrived home. I'd already decided to keep it there during the day until I could afford an actual gun safe. At night, I would keep it close to my bed, until I felt like my family's lives were out of danger, which I hoped would be soon.

As I was about to leave the bedroom, my cell phone rang. I dug it out of my pocket and noticed that it was a private number. When I answered, there was only silence.

"Hello?" I repeated a second time.

As I was about to hang up I heard someone chuckle.

"Hello? Scott?"

"I'm watching you…" whispered a raspy male voice.

I hung up the phone and dropped it on the bed, staring at it in horror. After a few seconds, it started to ring, again.

"No," I pleaded. "Leave me alone."

Frightened, I stepped backwards and right into someone's arms. I opened up my mouth and unleashed a scream that would have woken the dead.

"Hey, hey, hey, Lindsey – it's just me," said Jake, releasing me. "Fuck, I'm sorry."

"What the hell?!" I hollered, tears in my eyes. "You scared the shit out of me! What are you doing in my house?"

He took a step back. "Your garage was open and I noticed your truck parked inside. I went and knocked at the front door, but you never answered. I was worried, so I let myself in. Jesus, I'm sorry for scaring you."

I let out a frustrated sigh and put a hand to my forehead. "No, *I'm* sorry for freaking out. I've been so tense lately."

He moved closer to me. "You're going through a lot of shit. I certainly don't blame you for freaking out."

I stared up into into his face and realized at that moment, he made me feel completely safe. He was confident, strong, and obviously street-smart. I decided to throw caution to the wind and tell him everything. There was no way I could protect my kids all by myself and the person threatening me was obviously getting a kick out of terrorizing me now, too. I needed him.

"I have something to tell you," I said. "It's been scaring the hell out of me."

His face grew serious. "Okay."

I grabbed his hand and pulled him out of my bedroom. "Let's go into the kitchen and discuss it. I don't trust either of us near a bed."

He laughed. "Well, I have a better idea, why don't you come over to my house. I just made lunch. In fact, that's why I came over, to invite you."

I smiled. "Really? You made lunch? I thought you weren't much of a cook."

"Okay, you've got me. I picked up some sandwiches from the deli up the road."

"Well now that I know you didn't make anything, how can I resist?" I teased.

He smacked my rear and chased me into the living room. "You think you're funny, don't you?" he said, grabbing my belt loop and pulling me towards him.

"Hey, you're the one who said you couldn't cook," I said.

He turned me around and smiled down at me wickedly. "I can cook, just not in the kitchen."

"Somehow, I think you could cook there, too," I said.

His eyes smoldered with desire. "Let's get out of here before I forget why I invited you to my place."

I raised my eyebrows. "Like I'm any safer at your house?"

"The truth is, you're not safe anywhere with me," he said.

I locked up the house and followed him over to his place. When we walked through the door, the first thing I noticed was how bare and uncluttered his home was.

"You don't have much for furniture," I said, glancing around his living room. There was a black leather sofa and a large sixty-inch television and a coffee table. No stylish lamps or end tables, no paintings, and definitely no interior decorations.

"I also have a king-sized bed and a dining table in my kitchen. What more does a bachelor need?" he answered with a cocky grin.

"Good point."

We walked through the living room straight into the kitchen, which was clean and simple.

"Have a seat," he said, pulling out one of his oak dinette chairs.

"Thank you."

"You're welcome. I hope you like chicken-almond croissant sandwiches?"

"Sounds lovely," I said.

"So," he said, grabbing a couple of plates from his cupboard. "Besides having sex with me, what else is scaring the hell out of you?"

I laughed out loud. "I'm not scared of having sex with you."

"Bullshit," he teased.

"I'm not scared, Jake."

He folded his arms across his chest and leaned back against the counter. "Then prove it."

I shook my head and smiled. "You're incorrigible."

He chuckled. "I've been called worse."

"I can imagine."

He stared at me for a minute and then turned back to the sandwiches. "So, tell me what's on your mind."

I folded my hands on the table and stared down at them. "Someone broke into my bedroom the other night."

His head whipped around. "What?"

I looked up at him. "It was a stranger, a man. He threatened me and my children."

"Why in the hell didn't you tell me this before?!" he hollered.

He was very angry but I understood why, especially being a cop. "He said he'd kill me."

His eyes blazed with fury. "Tell me *exactly* what happened."

I went over everything, except for the part about buying a gun. I wasn't sure how he'd react, being a cop and all.

"You think it was the guy from the other night? Tina's husband?"

I nodded. "Well, I think he hired someone to threaten me. The guy in my house was much bigger than Jerry."

He rubbed a hand over his face and then nodded. "Okay, I'll take care of it."

My eyes widened. "Take care of it? What does that mean, exactly?"

He shrugged. "The less you know, the better."

"What?"

"Lindsey, this guy is in law enforcement. Chances are the asshole helping him is, too. I'm going to have to take care of both parties involved."

My eyebrows shot up. "Take care of?"

He smiled grimly. "Like I said, the less you know, the better."

"You're not talking about murder?" I whispered hoarsely.

He didn't answer me.

"Jake?"

His face darkened. "That guy threatened you with a knife. Now he's terrorizing you in other ways. He needs to be stopped and chances are he won't do it; even if I ask nicely."

"But," I sputtered, still in shock. "Can't you just *arrest* them?"

He raised his hands. "Do you have any evidence?"

I sighed. "I guess not."

He walked over to me and lifted my chin "Don't go worrying your pretty little head about it. In fact, just forget about this conversation completely."

I stared at him incredulously. "Right."

He turned my chair and then knelt down in front of me. "Lindsey. I'm not going to promise that someone won't get hurt. What I am going to promise is that it isn't going to be you, or your children."

"I just can't condone…"

He put a finger over my lips. "Uh-uh…forget about everything but the lunch I'm going to serve you."

I bit the side of my lip, wondering what kind of man Jake really was. Part of me wanted him to do exactly what he was hinting at, while the other side of me knew that I'd never be able to live with the guilt.

"Don't worry," he whispered. "I know what I'm doing."

I leaned forward and stared into his eyes. "Let me get this straight, you're actually talking about murder?"

"Well, I never really said 'murder', now did I?" he answered, with a straight face.

I tilted my head and nodded. "Fair enough. Then you'll just make sure they leave me alone without resorting to 'murder'?"

He smiled evenly. "I will make sure that your family is safe and that's all you really need to know."

I sighed in relief, still unable to believe the conversation we were having. "Well, thank you."

"You know, I'm going to expect a reward."

I raised my eyebrows. "Oh really?"

His eyes drifted over my body. "In fact, now that I finally have you in my lair, I think I'll collect on it right now."

Before I could respond, he lifted me out of the chair and set me directly on the table top.

"What are you doing?" I whispered.

"Showing you how 'good' being 'bad' can feel."

"I…"

His mouth captured mine, locking my lips so I couldn't protest. Then he slid his warm tongue into mine and began exploring my mouth. As our tongues began to tangle, I moaned into his mouth.

He released my lips. "You're driving me crazy, you know," he whispered, sliding his hands under my top. "You've consumed my every thought. This has never happened before."

The next thing I knew, my shirt was over my head and on the floor.

"Really?" I answered, staring up into his smoldering eyes as he pushed me all the way down with my back against the table.

"Yes, really. Jesus, you're so beautiful," he murmured, unclasping the front of my bra. He lowered his mouth and seized one of my nipples, rolling it around with his tongue, sending delicious tingles all the way down to my crotch.

I gasped and slipped my hands into his hair, pulling and twirling the short strands through my fingers as he moved to the other nipple, teasing and sucking the puckered tip.

"Hope you don't mind," he whispered, moving his hand to the button of my jeans. "but I need to taste you, all over."

OhmyGod...

Before I could stop him, he pulled my jeans off.

"Jake, wait…" I pleaded, as he slipped his hand under my panties. "I…Oh," I gasped, as he slid two fingers inside of me.

"You're so wet," he whispered, rubbing the pad of his thumb on my most sensitive spot.

"Yes," I breathed as he slid my panties to the side and replaced his thumb with his tongue, licking and sucking while I moaned in pleasure. I closed my eyes and gripped the edge of the table with my hands as it began to shake.

Noticing the table wobble, he wrapped my legs around his neck and pulled me closer to his face.

"Oh…God…" I whimpered as his fingers slide in and out of me.

"Say my name," he demanded, sucking greedily.

"Jake," I moaned.

"Baby, you taste so good," he whispered, reaching up to caress one of my breasts.

My body was on fire as his tongue danced around my labia and his fingers continued their glorious assault. I closed my eyes and gripped the muscles of his arms, digging my nails into the skin.

"Fuck, Lindsey, you turn me on."

Hearing his deep, sexy voice say my name brought me over the edge. "Oh, yes!" I screamed as my stomach clenched up and I came longer and harder than I could ever remember. After a few more strokes of his tongue, it became too intense and I tried pushing him away, but he held me down until he was satisfied with the results.

"Wow," I breathed as my legs finally stopped trembling.

He raised his head and gave me a devilish grin. "You know what? I guess I *can* hold my own in the kitchen."

Before I could agree, someone rang the doorbell.

"Perfect timing," he grunted, standing up.

I scrambled off of the table and rushed to get my clothes back on. "Were you expecting anyone?" I asked.

He washed his hands and headed towards the living room. "Nope. Wait right here."

A minute later, he walked back into the kitchen with a grim expression on his face.

"Who was it?" I asked.

"Couple of cops," he said. "They're looking for you."

Chapter Twenty-one

I quickly followed him to the front door where two men dressed in suits stood outside, waiting.

"Are you Lindsey Shepard?" asked the taller of the two, his dark blue eyes regarding me coolly.

"Yes," I answered, crossing my arms under my chest. "What's this about and how in the world did you even know I was here?"

"The neighbor from across the street told us," replied the other cop with a smug look on his face. "We weren't interrupting anything?"

I stared at nosy old Mrs. Hanson who was watching us from her garden. "We were having lunch, actually."

The tall detective flashed me his badge. "Sorry to interrupt your meal. I'm Detective Reed Parker and this is my partner, Dave Franklin."

I nodded. "What can I do for you?"

"When was the last time you spoke to your husband?" asked Detective Parker. "Scott Shepard."

Scott? Lord, what has he gotten himself into now?

"Last night. Around four o'clock."

He took out a notepad and began writing.

"So, yesterday around four o'clock was the last time you had any contact with him? Did he happen to say where he was going afterwards?"

I shook my head. "No."

Detective Parker glanced at Jake again and frowned. "You know, I think it would be better if we interview you alone, Mrs. Shepard."

"Can you tell us what's going on here?" interrupted Jake.

Parker's lips thinned. "We'll get into that momentarily with Mrs. Shepard, although I'm starting to think we should interview you, too, since you're their neighbor. What was your name?"

"Jake Sharp."

Parker frowned. "Jake Sharp? That name sounds familiar."

"It very well might. I work in Narcotics," said Jake. "The North Central Drug Task Force, to be specific. We've probably crossed paths before."

Parker's eyebrows shot up. "Do you have I.D.?"

Jake reached into his back pocket and took out his wallet. "I just moved here a few months ago," he said, flashing his badge. "Before that, I worked in the Hennepin County Task Force, in Minnesota."

Parker glanced at the badge and then nodded. "Okay, well I'd definitely like to talk to you some more. First and foremost, however, Mrs.

Shepard, can we take a walk back over to your house to speak in private?"

I nodded. "Of course."

"I'm coming with," said Jake.

Parker held up his hand. "No offense, but we really need to talk to her alone. You understand."

Jake nodded, reluctantly. "Fine. But, remember, I'm here if you need me, Lindsey."

I smiled weakly. "Okay."

I could feel Jake's eyes on me as I followed the detectives back to my home. It was very obvious that he didn't like taking orders from anyone, let alone two other cops.

"Would you like some coffee or anything?" I asked, as they followed me into the kitchen.

Parker shook his head. "No, I'm fine."

"I'm good, too," said the other cop. He was a short, squat man with a bulbous nose and beady little eyes. Parker, on the other hand, looked more like a television version of an investigator. He was attractive with dazzling blue eyes, wavy blonde hair, and a five o'clock shadow. There was no doubt in my mind that if Darcy was here, she'd be investigating him.

"Alright," I sighed. "So, what has Scott done?"

"Why do you think Scott's done something?" asked Parker.

"Well, then why are you here?" I asked, getting more frustrated by the minute. They were stalling and it was starting to really piss me off.

"Please sit down, Mrs. Shepard," said Parker, pointing towards my kitchen table.

"Call me Lindsey," I replied, sitting down.

Parker sat across from me while the other detective leaned back against the center island, watching us.

"Lindsey," said Parker, rubbing a hand over his chin. "Look, there's no easy way to break this to you, but your husband, Scott Shepard, was found murdered earlier this morning."

I felt like someone had kicked me in the stomach. I stared at him in horror as he studied my reaction.

"What did you say?" I asked in a strangled voice.

Parker sighed and took out his notepad again. "He was found in his car, a bullet wound to the back of the head."

"Oh, my God," I choked, tears flooding my eyes, making him a blur of blue and gray. I shook my head. "No – I just can't believe that!"

The other detective grabbed a paper towel from the counter and handed it to me as the tears ran down my cheeks. "I'm sorry," he said. "It's true. We'll need you to come down to the morgue and verify that it's him."

"Maybe it isn't," I squeaked, my eyes darting from one to the other. "I just can't believe someone would kill him. Are you certain?"

Parker nodded. "We believe it is. His wallet was left on him, containing his driver's license. But, obviously, we'll still need you to I.D. him."

"Why would someone kill him?" I asked, wiping my tears with the coarse paper towel.

Parker sighed. "That's what we're trying to find out, Mrs. Shepard. They didn't take his wallet, so we can rule out burglary. He had over one hundred dollars and a bunch of credit cards."

"Not even a robbery?" I mumbled.

"No, it could have been just a random killing or something more. Did your husband use drugs?" asked Parker.

I shook my head. "Not that I know of."

"We talked with his secretary," said Detective Franklin. "She mentioned that you two had recently separated?"

"Yes, just a couple of weeks ago, actually."

Parker nodded. "So, you weren't getting along?"

I narrowed my eyes. "We were getting along fine," I snapped, realizing where this might be heading.

"Take it easy," said Parker with a little smile. "We aren't accusing you of anything. We have to eliminate you as a suspect and to do that, we have to do some digging. I'm sorry if it makes you uncomfortable."

I stared at the paper towel and nodded. "Okay. I guess I understand that."

"It's just procedure," said Franklin.

Parker glanced at Franklin and then back to me. "So, if you were getting along fine, why did you separate?"

I sighed. "Because he cheated on me."

"Cheated? Well, that must have made you angry," said Franklin.

I nodded. "It was very painful. I walked in on him with two other women. He claimed that he was 'coerced' into it."

The look on Parker's face was a mixture of shock and amusement. "He actually said he was *coerced*?"

"I know…right?" I said, managing a bitter smile. "I thought it was a pretty pathetic excuse as well."

"It's definitely an imaginative excuse. One I haven't personally heard before," said Franklin, shaking his head.

"Here's an idea, why don't you question the women he was screwing around with?" I mumbled. "Maybe they have husbands who found out and weren't too happy. One of them may have flipped out and killed him."

"Well, we'll definitely look into that," said Parker, writing more notes onto his notepad.

"So, where was he killed?" I asked, blinking back more tears as the reality of what had happened was starting to really sink in. I still couldn't believe he was dead. The man I'd been married to and had loved at one time with all of my heart was gone forever. Even after everything that had happened in the last couple of weeks, I still cared about him. And now he was gone and there was nothing for us to work out.

What in the name of God would I tell our children?

"He was found in the parking ramp at his place of employment," said Parker.

I nodded. "Well, he *was* always at the office."

"So, what's going on with you and your neighbor?" asked Franklin.

My eyes shot over to him and I could tell by the smug look on his face, he definitely suspected something illicit.

"We're friends."

"Both of you looked a little disheveled when we showed up," he replied, "like we interrupted more than just lunch."

"He's a good neighbor and friend who invited me to lunch," I retorted, glaring at him.

"Calm down," said Parker. "So, you're friends. It's good to have friends."

"Damn right, it is," I agreed.

"Mrs. Shepard, did you kill your husband?" asked Franklin, staring at me like a cat would a canary.

Chapter Twenty-two

I knew the question would come but I was still unprepared for the way it affected me. "No!" I choked, staring at him in horror. "I loved Scott and would never hurt him, let alone kill him!"

Parker nodded slowly. "Okay. Can you tell us where you were from around nine o'clock last night until around seven o'clock this morning?"

"I was here, sleeping in my bed."

"Are there witnesses?" asked Franklin.

I stared at Franklin with something close to loathing. "My children can verify that I was home."

"What about when they were sleeping? Can anyone else verify that you were around?" asked Franklin.

"No, I guess not," I said, my lips trembling. "But let me tell *you* something, Detective Franklin, I *loved* my husband, even after he cheated on me. I loved him and would never have done anything to harm him. I'm not a violent person, you can ask anyone."

Franklin and Parker exchanged a look and I fought hard to control my rage. Somehow, I knew I was still a suspect.

Parker stood up. "Well, I think that's enough for now. We'll need access to his home computer and then check his office and interview his co-workers."

"You can take his computer, as far as I'm concerned. I have my own and couldn't care less about Scott's."

Parker nodded. "That would be very helpful. We'll return it after we've gone through it, though."

"Fine."

"Would you like a ride to the morgue, Mrs. Shepard?" asked Parker.

The thought of spending any more time with them left a sour taste in my mouth. "No. I'll find a ride, thank you."

"We'll definitely keep in touch," said Franklin, still studying me. "Don't leave town."

"Of course not," I replied, coldly. "I want to make sure you catch the person responsible for murdering Scott, even more than you do."

"We'll try our best to put that person behind bars. It was nice meeting you," said Parker, holding out his hand. "Sorry it was under such horrible circumstances."

I nodded and shook his hand, avoiding Franklin's outstretched one, as if by accident. The thought of touching him made my skin crawl.

"We're going next door to talk with your *good* neighbor, see if he saw your husband leaving last night or noticed anything unusual," said Franklin.

"Be my guest," I said, walking them to the door.

"If you remember anything unusual, call us," said Parker, handing me his business card.

"I certainly will, Detective."

Parker raised his finger. "Oh, and you'll probably start getting bombarded by the media. Just tell them 'no comment' when they start hounding you. Eventually, they'll go away."

I sighed. "Wonderful. I didn't even think about that."

Once they left, I sat down in a recliner and erupted into fresh wave of tears, crying for Scott, our children, and all of the precious memories we'd had before everything went to hell. I also scolded myself for messing around with Jake and wondered if Scott would still be alive if I would have only let him back into our home.

As I thought about all of the "what ifs", my phone began to ring. I grabbed it and stared at the unknown number, almost afraid to answer it. I could barely talk as it was, and I didn't want to answer any more questions about Scott. But, I also knew there were a lot of people that I had to contact, including his parents, my mother, and our friends. I took a deep breath and answered.

"Lindsey," sobbed Molly.

I closed my eyes. "You've heard."

"Yes, oh God – my son is dead. I just don't know what to do," she moaned.

I sighed. "Molly, is Henry there with you?"

"Yes, he's on the other phone trying to call the investigators who are handling the case."

"Well, two of them just left here," I said.

"Oh. Lindsey, do the children know yet?" she asked.

"No." I shuddered at the thought of telling them. "They're still at school."

"Those poor children! I just can't believe it," she sobbed. "It sounds so ridiculous, someone murdered him? He was a good man, I just don't understand…"

"I know," I said. "Molly, I have to get ready to go to the morgue."

Molly started wailing at the mention of the morgue.

"I'm sorry, Molly," I said through her sobs. "I really have to go."

"Wait – we can give you a ride," she said, blowing her nose. "I want to make sure it's really Scott."

Although I loved Scott's parents, I wasn't prepared to deal with Molly. She was a very high-strung woman and the thought of being near her now was just too exhausting.

"I'll just meet you out there," I said. "I have a ride."

"Okay, honey," she said, blowing her nose. "What Henry? Oh – Henry says we should be there around three."

"Well, I guess I'll see you then," I said.

After I hung up with her I called Darcy and left her a voicemail. Then I called my mother.

"What? Oh, my Lord, Lindsey! Somebody actually shot him?" she cried.

I sighed. "Yes, that's what they're telling me."

"Well," she said. "I'm taking the first flight out. Don't even think about arguing this one with me."

I ran a hand through my hair and nodded. "Okay. Let me know when your flight arrives and I'll pick you up."

"No, I'll just rent a car. I'm not going to be an inconvenience and I'll need one to use when I'm out there anyway. Besides, you have too much to deal with right now."

I closed my eyes. *Yes, I'm now a widow.*

"Mom," I cried softly. "I just can't believe it. I keep thinking it's a nightmare and I'm going to wake up any minute."

She sighed. "Honey, I'm so sorry for the pain you must be feeling. I know how much you loved Scott. Even with everything that was going on."

I nodded. "I guess part of me still did."

"Everything will work out," she said. "I'm going to book a flight and I'll let you know when I'll be arriving."

"Okay."

"I love you, honey."

"I love you, too, mom."

I hung up with her and less than two minutes later, Darcy returned my call.

"Oh, my God, Lindsey, are you okay?"

"I'm still in shock," I mumbled. "I just can't believe it. Who would kill Scott?"

"I hate to say this," she said. "But he may have kept a lot more from you than just his affairs. Didn't you say he was behind on the bills as well? Maybe he owed someone money and they were tired of waiting…"

"Oh, Jesus, I never even considered that," I said.

What *had* crossed my mind was the guy who'd been threatening me. I wondered if he'd killed Scott as a warning to me. I'd even thought of mentioning it to the investigators, but the niggling voice in the back of my head kept warning me to keep quiet. If he did kill my husband, he might also murder my children. I didn't know who to trust. Not even the police.

"What about drugs?" she asked. "Do you know if he was into any?"

"I guess it's possible. If you would have asked me two weeks ago, I would have said *absolutely* not. But after these last few days, I really have no idea."

After a few more consoling words, she agreed to take me to the morgue.

"Of course I'll take you. I'll be over shortly," she said. "I just have to make a phone call and then I'll shoot over."

"Thanks Darcy."

I hung up, went into the bathroom and looked in the mirror. My face was puffy from the tears and I looked horrible. I grabbed my makeup bag and started applying some concealer under my eyes, but it wasn't much help and I soon just gave up. As I washed the makeup from my hands, the doorbell rang.

"Come on in," I said to Jake, stepping aside. "We wouldn't want the neighbors gossiping any more than they already are."

"Fuck the other neighbors," he said.

I rubbed my forehead and sighed.

"So," he said. "Are you okay?"

My eyes filled back with tears. "I have to go down and identify my husband's body," I answered.

"I figured as much."

"I just can't believe this is happening," I said.

He reached out and brushed a tear from my cheek. "Would you like me to come with you?"

I cleared my throat. "No, thank you. Darcy is taking me."

He nodded slowly. "Okay."

"Look," I said, looking down. "Earlier today – it was great, but…"

He tilted his head. "But what?"

"It's not a good time. In fact, I think we should back off of whatever it is we've started."

He stared at me for a few seconds and then nodded. "I understand. You're going through a lot of shit right now. You need time to sort things out."

I shook my head. "Jake, it's more than that. I just can't get involved with you. In fact, I shouldn't have led you on in the first place."

He frowned. "You didn't lead me on."

"But I didn't say 'no' either. That was my fault."

He folded his arms across his chest. "You haven't done anything wrong; quit being so hard on yourself."

I ignored him. "You're a great looking guy with a lot to offer someone and I'm not ready for anything right now. My kids need to come first, and I just…"

He stared at me through his thick, dark lashes. "Just what…don't have time for me?"

"I'm sorry. It may sound cold, but my kids need me now more than ever. I have to be there for them."

"Lindsey," he said, leaning forward. "You're in mourning and not thinking clearly. I'll give you time, but I want you to know, I'm here for you and I'm definitely not going anywhere."

I realized he wasn't really listening to me, and that it was pointless to argue, so I just nodded.

He sighed. "Okay, I'm going to call you later to see how you're doing. Remember, I'm right next door if you need anything."

"Um…my mother's flying down and Darcy will be here. I'm sure I'll be fine."

"Good," he said. "Now, about that other problem we talked about. I'm going to take care of it while you deal with this."

I nodded.

"If you get any more threats in the meantime, let me know."

I nodded.

His hand snaked out and grabbed my wrist. "Lindsey," he said, staring into my eyes. "I'm serious as all hell. These guys are probably responsible for Scott's death. It's too much of a coincidence."

"I wondered about that myself."

"Did you tell the investigators anything?"

I shook my head. "No."

He released my arm. "Good. Don't trust anyone else with this information. I've already made a few phone calls and found out that Jerry has other family members working in different areas of the police force."

I rolled my eyes. "Great."

He nodded. "He has a cousin named Gary and a couple of step-brothers. I'm inclined to believe that Gary might be the guy fucking with you. My informant tells me he's a real asshole."

I bit the side of my lip. "I wonder if you can get me a picture of him. I want to see if it's the guy from the restaurant."

"I'll see what I can do."

"Thanks, Jake. I don't know what I'd do without your help."

He squeezed my hand. "I'm just glad I'm able to offer it."

I nodded. "Well, Darcy should be here any minute. I'd better finish getting ready."

"Okay," he said, leaning forward to kiss me.

"Please don't," I said, placing my hand on his chest.

He touched my stomach with his fingertips and it made my stomach all fluttery. "That's fine," he whispered, "for now. But if you think I'm going to walk away that easily, you don't know me that well. I realize you're mourning for Scott, but don't forget the pain he caused you. I'd never hurt you like that."

"Jake."

He silenced me with a hard kiss. When he released me, his mouth twisted into a satisfied grin. "See, this isn't over, not by a long shot," he said, backing away. "I'm not giving up on you."

I stared at him, unable to speak, as he turned and went back to his house.

Chapter Twenty-three

Darcy showed up when I was on the phone with my mother.

"Is she coming out here?" asked Darcy as I hung up.

I nodded. "She'll be here sometime after nine o'clock tonight."

"Will she need a ride from the airport?"

I shook my head. "No, she's going to rent a car. She doesn't want to be an inconvenience, she claims."

"Sounds like her," smiled Darcy. "How are you holding up?"

I sighed. "I'm still in shock. The kids will be home in an hour and I don't know how in the hell I'm going to tell them."

"I'll help you," she murmured, giving me a hug. "You don't have to do this alone."

"Thanks."

"I suppose we should get going," said Darcy, pulling away.

I nodded and then left a note for the kids, telling them I'd be back soon.

***

On the way to the morgue, I wanted to believe that the detectives had made a tragic mistake. That Scott was busy at work or even hiding out in a hotel somewhere, screwing one of his clients. But when they showed me the body, there was no mistaking that it was him, even with the horrific bullet wound.

"Molly shouldn't see this," I said to Darcy in a strangled voice as we walked out of the examining room. "Nobody should have to remember a loved one that way."

"Isn't that the truth? Speaking of which – I wonder where his parents are?" asked Darcy, looking at her watch.

"They're probably getting interviewed by the cops," I said. "The investigators seem to have this notion that I killed Scott."

Darcy snorted. "Stupid idiots. They obviously have their heads up their asses."

"I know…right?" I said, shaking my head. "I tell you what, these last few weeks have been the worst times of my life and it just keeps getting worse."

She squeezed my shoulder. "I know, hon. I wish there was something I could do."

"You've done more than enough already," I said.

After verifying that the deceased was indeed Scott, we met with a member of the local church clergy who prayed with us. As we were ending the prayer, I heard Molly's wails coming from the examining room. Apparently, my in-laws had also verified that it was Scott's body.

Darcy cringed. "I guess mom and dad have arrived."

Two minutes later, a distraught Henry helped his wife into the morgue's "Grieving Room" and we exchanged hugs.

"How could this have happened?" choked Molly, wiping her eyes with a tissue. "Scott was such a good man."

"I know," I said as fresh tears filled my eyes.

"Have they found anything out, yet?" asked Darcy.

Henry shook his head. "They don't have any witnesses and not much to go on. Detective Parker is going to stay in touch with me, however."

I cleared my throat. I didn't want to bring it up, but I was curious. "Did Scott tell you exactly why we were separated?"

"He didn't get into specifics," said Henry. "But from what I understood, he'd screwed up pretty big, and you needed some space to think things through."

I nodded, not wanting to bring the sordid details in front of Molly.

"I have to go," I said. "The children are probably home by now and they need to be told."

"Of course," said Henry. "Molly and I were wondering if the children could still come and stay with us tomorrow night? I think having them close will be especially good for Molly," he said, motioning towards her, although from the look in his eyes, he needed Scott's children close to him just as much.

"Of course," I murmured. "I'll call you tomorrow."

We hugged once more and then Darcy drove me back home. The ride back was somber and I stared out the window, wondering how I was going to break it to the children.

When we pulled up to the house, Jake was in his yard, cutting the grass. He killed the engine when he saw us, but I avoided making eye contact.

"Damn that man is fine," stated Darcy as she followed me onto the porch. "Every time I see him, I just want to jump his bones."

I didn't respond. What had happened between us was one thing I wasn't prepared to share with her, just yet.

As we entered the house, I could hear Regan on the phone, laughing with one of her friends. What I was about to do tore me apart.

"How do I do this?" I whispered.

Darcy grabbed my hand and squeezed. "You just have to tell them the truth. They'll certainly hear about it on television, so the sooner they hear about it from their *mother*, the better."

"Jesus, I didn't even think about that," I said, as we walked into the kitchen.

Regan was sitting at the dinette, smiling into her cell phone and Jeremy was stuffing his face with macaroni and cheese while leafing through a *Victoria's Secret* catalog.

Jeremy looked up and closed the catalog. "Oh, hey, mom. Hey, Darcy."

I forced a smile. "Hi, honey."

His eyes narrowed. "What's wrong?"

I cleared my throat. "Regan, honey, get off the phone. I have something to tell you."

She held up a finger, telling me to wait. Then she burst out laughing at something the caller said.

"Have you been crying?" asked Jeremy incredulously.

Regan's eyes shot over to mine. "Crap, I have to go," she mumbled into the phone and then hung up.

I stared at my children, my lips trembling. "I have something very unfortunate to tell you."

"What?" asked Jeremy.

Darcy grabbed my hand and squeezed it.

"I...um...your dad's no longer with us," I said, my voice breaking.

Regan rolled her eyes. "We know that, he moved out almost two weeks ago."

I shook my head and the floodgates opened back up. "No, kids, your dad, he's...dead."

"What?!" cried Regan.

"That's a lie," argued Jeremy. "We just saw him last night."

Regan flung herself at me and I held her in my arms. "It's true," I said. "He was killed."

"Killed?" choked Jeremy.

I held out my other hand and soon all three of us were holding each other and crying while Darcy stood watching, tears streaming down her cheeks as well.

"What happened?" asked Jeremy

We pulled apart and I stared in sorrow at my children. "The only thing I really know is that someone shot him in his car. It might have been a random killing; they're not even really sure why he was murdered."

"Oh, poor Daddy," wept Regan.

"So they don't know who killed him, yet?" asked Jeremy.

I shook my head. "No, but I'm sure they'll figure it out, Jeremy. They'll catch this person and put him away."

His eyes filled with fury. "I hope they find his killer and they get the death penalty."

I sighed, understanding his feelings. It was hard enough for me to deal with but I couldn't even begin to imagine what it was like for the kids. Scott had been a great father and they'd loved him dearly.

"I'm going up to my room," said Regan, brushing tears from her cheeks. "I just want to lie down for a while."

I released her hand. "Okay."

"I'm going to my room, too," mumbled Jeremy.

I walked over to him and gave him another hug. "We'll get through this," I said. "We will."

His body started to shake as I held him and soon he was sobbing all over again. I closed my eyes and prayed that we'd somehow get through this.

"Crap," said Darcy when her phone began to vibrate. She took it out of her purse and frowned. "I have to go, Lindsey. I'm sorry."

I turned around to face her. "It's no problem at all. Thanks for everything, Darcy."

"Call me later," she said, squeezing my shoulder.

I nodded. "I will."

"Come here, Jeremy," she said, giving him a hug. "Just remember, *you're* the man of the house now. In fact, I bet your dad's looking down at you with a proud smile on his face, knowing very well that you can handle this."

He wiped his cheeks and nodded.

"Chin up," she said, her gaze shifting between us. "*Both* of you."

"Yes, ma'am," I said.

"Bye, Darcy," said Jeremy.

I walked her to the door and thanked her again for being such a rock.

"No problem, honey. It's what friends are for. Oh," she said, putting a hand against her forehead. "I forgot to tell you, I sent your resume to that Sheriff I was telling you about. Anyway, he's going to give you a call next week," she smiled. "To schedule an interview."

A job interview was the last thing on my mind. I sighed. "Okay."

She touched my shoulder. "It might not be the best time for this, but it could be your financial answer. Unless, Scott left you some life insurance?"

I shrugged. "Frankly, I have no idea."

"Well, funerals don't pay for themselves, so I'd check on that soon."

I nodded.

"Let me know when your mom arrives," she said.

"Okay."

After she left, I sat on the couch with Jeremy for a while and we talked about Scott, reminiscing about much better times. Soon Regan came back down and joined us. As the sun went down, I stood up and stretched.

"I'd better make dinner," I said, looking at my watch.

"I'm starving," said Jeremy. "Can we just order a pizza or something?"

I smiled. "You know, that sounds like a great plan."

I made a phone call, and a half hour later, the pizza man showed up with a large pepperoni and mushroom pie. When I handed him my credit card for verification, he frowned.

"Didn't they call you back?" he asked. "The card was declined."

I sighed. "No, nobody called me back."

"I'm sorry, ma'am. We'll need another form of payment. It's fifteen ninety-eight."

"I'll take care of it," said Jake, climbing the steps.

I raised my eyebrows. "Where'd you come from?"

He wiggled his eyebrows. "I was lurking in the shadows when I heard the cry from a damsel in distress."

I smiled. "You goof."

He handed the pizza man a twenty and told him to keep the change."

"Thank you," I said after the young man left. "I'll pay you back, later."

His eyes twinkled. "You know how I prefer my payments."

I frowned. "Jake..."

He chuckled. "Sorry, I couldn't' resist."

"Well, thanks," I said. "I'd ask you to join us, but it's not a good time."

"That's okay, I was just leaving."

He was dressed in black jeans and a black sweatshirt. Not his normal work attire.

"You working?"

"Something like that."

From the look on his face, I wondered if it had to do with my stalker situation. I shivered at the thought. "Oh."

"Well, have a good night," he said.

"Be careful. Please."

"Don't worry about me."

I looked down at his hand, the bandage was gone. "Your hand must be doing better?"

He raised it in the air and nodded. "It's okay."

I grimaced. "Are those teeth marks?"

He shrugged.

I sighed. "Please come back unscathed."

Jake smiled and then looked beyond my shoulder. "Hey, Jeremy."

"Hi, Jake," said Jeremy. "Mom, come on, we're starving in here."

"Sorry. Well, thanks again, Jake. I'll pay you back as soon as possible."

A smile curled on one side of his mouth. "Oh, I know you will."

I felt a rush of heat at the way he was staring at me and groaned inwardly. My body, as usual, was my own worst enemy. "Goodbye, Jake," I said.

"See you later," he answered as I shut the door.

I brought the pizza to the kitchen just as my cell phone started to ring.

My mother.

"Hi."

"I'm on my way to your place now from the airport," she answered. "I just rented a car and should be there in about a half hour. Do you need anything?"

I licked my some tomato a sauce from my finger. "No thanks, mom. We just had a pizza delivered; I'll try and save you some."

She snorted. "Good grief, my acid reflux won't be able to handle that. I'll find something else."

I smiled. "Okay, see you soon."

"Grandma's in town?" asked Regan after I hung up.

I nodded. "Yes."

"Awesome," she replied. "I've missed her so much."

"I do too, honey."

I dished out the pizza and we ate in silence. When we were finished, I turned on the radio and began loading the dishwasher.

"Mom, you have a phone call," said Regan, walking into the kitchen.

I dried my hands off. "I didn't even hear it ring."

She sighed. "That's because I was on the phone when they beeped in. Anyway, the man said it couldn't wait and that he just *had* to talk to you, now. Let me know when you're done so I can call my friend back."

"Why can't you use your cell phone?"

"Because, I don't want to waste my minutes."

"Okay," I said, taking the cordless phone from her. "Hello?"

"Stupid bitch – I told you to keep your mouth shut," rasped a familiar deep voice. "The next time you open it, I'm going to murder your kids while you watch, and then fuck you until you beg for death."

He hung up and I stared at the phone in horror.

Chapter Twenty-four

"Mom, what is it?" asked Regan.

"I...um...it's nothing," I said, trying to remain calm, although my hands were shaking when I handed her back the phone.

Regan frowned. "Was it something about dad?"

Unable to look her directly in the eye, I shook my head and walked away. "No. I'll be right back."

"But..."

I left the kitchen, grabbed my cell phone from my purse, and called Jake. Now that my suspicions were confirmed, I was more terrified than ever. Unfortunately, he didn't answer.

"Hi, it's Lindsey. Please call me as soon as you can," I said, leaving a message.

"Mom, grandma's here!" yelled Regan.

I took a deep breath and tried to collect myself as I walked into the living room.

"Lindsey," sighed my mother, taking me in her arms. "My poor baby."

I closed my eyes and inhaled her familiar vanilla scent. "Hi, mom," I murmured.

She took a step back and stared at me. "Well, you certainly look good. I see you've lost some weight and had your hair done?"

I sighed. "The weight wasn't on purpose but the hair was."

"Well, stress becomes you, dear."

"Gee, thanks," I snorted.

"Jeremy, can you help me with my bags?" she asked as he entered the living room.

He sighed. "Sure."

"Regan can you help your brother?" I asked.

"Fine," she grumbled.

"Typical teenagers," said my mother as they trudged out the door. "Any kind of physical labor just about kills them."

"You look good," I said to her.

She patted her short red hair and smiled. "Thanks, I had my hair done, too."

You could definitely tell she and I were mother and daughter, except for our body types. She was rail thin where my curves were still borderline chubby, even after losing ten pounds these last couple of weeks.

"Have you talked to your sister?" she asked.

I sighed. "No, I didn't want to bother her with any of this. But now that Scott's dead, I suppose I should call her."

"Well, I can certainly call her for you," she said. "In fact, why don't you go lie down and I'll get everyone settled for the night?"

"Actually, I'm going to go for a drive," I said. "I just need to get out of the house for a little while. I won't be gone long; then we can talk."

She nodded. "Okay. I guess I can understand that."

The truth of the matter was I wanted to drive by Tina's place to see if anything was going on. I'd avoided driving by that area ever since the threats had started.

I tried calling Jake again as I drove off in the SUV, but there was still no answer, which started to worry me. What if something horrible had happened to him? He was obviously placing himself in a lot of danger.

For me.

I left him another message. "Please call me. I'm getting worried."

Sighing, I turned towards Tina's home and then was surprised to see a "For Sale" sign in the front yard. As I slowed down, my phone began to ring.

"Jake," I said.

"Missed me?"

"I received a phone call from the guy who's been threatening me," I said. "He made it pretty clear that he was the one who killed Scott."

Jake swore. "I was afraid of that."

"What am I going to do? I'm so scared."

"I just got home. Can you come over and we'll talk?"

I sighed. "I'm driving around at the moment."

He was silent.

"Jake?"

"Where are you?"

"I just passed Tina's home. Did you know they have their house up for sale?"

"I just found out myself. They've already moved out."

"Did you find them?" I asked.

"We'll talk about it when you get back here."

"Okay. I have to check back in with my mom first, she's staying with me."

"Okay."

I hung up and headed home. When I arrived back at the house, my mom was in her nightgown and yawning.

"Honey, I'm just exhausted. I shouldn't have stayed up drinking last night. I don't know what I was thinking. Would you mind if we talked tomorrow?"

"No, that's fine. I'm going over to the neighbor's house for a little while, anyway."

She raised her eyebrows. "The neighbor?"

I nodded. "He's a police officer and is trying to help with the case."

She walked over and gave me a hug. "Okay, dear. Don't stay up too late."

"I won't."

After she went to bed, I went upstairs and checked on the kids, who were thankfully both sleeping. Then I walked over to Jake's.

"Hey," he said, holding the door open for me. I could hear *Bob Seger* playing in the background and there were two empty beer bottles on the hardwood floor, next to his sofa.

"So, what's going on?" I asked as we stood in the living room, staring at each other.

He cleared his throat. "I'll get to that in a second. Would you like a beer or glass of wine? I picked some up at the liquor store."

"Sure, what kind of wine do you have?"

"A Merlot or Moscato?"

"I'll take a glass of the Moscato. Thank you."

"You're welcome. Sit down and make yourself at home," he said, walking towards the kitchen looking sexy as always, this time in a tight grey Harley T-shirt and faded blue jeans.

I sank into the sofa and closed my eyes as another song started. Two minutes later, Jake walked out of the kitchen with a tall goblet of white wine and another beer for himself.

I smiled as he handed me the wine. "This is a pretty big glass. You're not trying to get me drunk, are you, Detective Sharp?"

He sat down next to me and put his feet up on the coffee table. "That depends on if it makes you easy."

I laughed. "You just don't give up, do you?"

He chuckled. "Now that I've had a taste, I want more. What can I say?"

Remembering our interlude in the kitchen, I felt my cheeks heat up. "Would you just stop?"

"You're no fun," he pouted.

I took a sip of my wine. "Did you find out anything?"

He took a swig of his beer and nodded. "Yeah, I found Tina and her husband."

My eyes widened. "And..?"

He's in the hospital."

"Oh, my God – did you put him there?"

He laughed. "Unfortunately, no, he's been in the hospital for a couple of days. Appendicitis."

I released a heavy sigh. "So, he's not the one who killed Scott?"

"No. But I did talk to Tina."

"What did she have to say?"

He rubbed his chin. "Not much."

I closed my eyes and groaned.

"Hey," he said. "It's okay. I didn't think she would anyway. But don't worry, I found what I needed on my own."

My eyebrows shot up. "How?"

He smiled. "It's a secret. If I told you, I'd have to…"

"Kill me?" I interrupted, taking another sip of the sweet wine.

"No," he replied, with a cocky grin. "I'd have to fuck you so hard, you'd forget."

His words, the memories of earlier, and the heat of the wine had an immediate effect. Before I could stop myself, I set my glass down and put a hand on his chest. "In that case, you'd better tell me."

He groaned and pulled me onto his lap. "Woman, you're not making this easy on me. How am I supposed to back off when you tease me like that?"

I lowered my eyes, wondering what the hell I was doing myself. I'd planned on keeping my distance but I just couldn't resist the man. "I don't know. I'm not even sure what I'm doing."

He lifted my chin and we stared into each other's eyes. "I swear to you, Lindsey, I won't fuck with your head."

I slipped my arms around his neck and pulled his lips to mine. "I know," I whispered into his mouth.

He slid his hands over my hips and pushed me against his hardness. "You sure about this?"

I wasn't.

But, I closed my eyes and pressed against him, enjoying the sensation. "Yes," I breathed as his lips moved to my neck.

He stood up with my legs wrapped around his waist and carried me down the hall to his bedroom. I glanced around and noted that it was also relatively simple, save for the luxurious king-sized bed and another large television mounted to the wall.

I sighed in pleasure when he dropped me onto the plush mattress. "Mm… I love your bed.

"Far as I'm concerned, a man's bed is just as important as his television. Now, last chance to back out – once I get you naked, I'm not stopping," he said, crawling towards me on the bed.

"I wouldn't want you to."

He stared into my eyes and touched my cheek. "Lindsey, do you trust me?"

I nodded. "Yes."

He leaned over me and pulled out something from his nightstand.

My eyes widened at the sight of handcuffs. "Oh…um, maybe we should use those another time?"

He smiled. "You said you trusted me."

"Yes, but…"

"No buts," he said, straddling my waist with his thighs. The next thing I knew, he had my arms above my head and they were handcuffed to the brushed metal headboard.

"I don't know about this," I whispered against his mouth as he began kissing me.

He raised his head and brushed a strand of hair from my cheek. "Relax."

I closed my eyes and sighed as his lips moved to my neck and his hands to my breasts.

"Now you're all mine," he said, unbuttoning my top and then removing my bra.

I moaned as his mouth found my nipples, licking and sucking the tips, causing a delicious ache below.

"Screw this, just let me touch you," I begged.

"You need to learn patience," he whispered, flicking and twirling his tongue around my nipple.

"Right," I breathed as his other hand slid down to my jeans and began unbuttoning them.

He chuckled. "I promise it'll be worth it."

"You're already driving me crazy," I whispered as he slipped a hand into my jeans.

"I've only started," he replied with a seductive smile. Then he lowered his face to my navel and began making a trail with his tongue towards the top of my panties.

"Oh, God…" I squeaked, wanting so badly to run my fingers through his hair.

"Let's get these out of the way," he whispered, tugging at my jeans. The next thing I knew they were off and I had nothing but my panties left.

"What about you?" I whispered.

"All in good time," he said, moving his hands to my thighs and separating them.

I closed my eyes and let out a ragged breath as his fingers slid under the cotton.

"See, I knew you'd enjoy this," he whispered, rubbing my sweet spot.

"Oh…I…Jesus…" I breathed as he buried his face between my legs and began pleasuring me. I arched my back as his strokes grew even wilder, feeling both torture and pleasure at being so vulnerable.

"Let's see if this makes it better," he whispered, sliding two fingers inside of me. Then his tongue moved back, licking me in a delicious frenzy and it took no time before my hips were bucking and an orgasm slammed through my body like a massive tidal wave.

"Yes…OhmyGod…Yes…" I gasped, wanting so badly to touch him. "Please!"

"Please what?" he asked, sliding his tongue back up towards my belly button.

"Take them off," I demanded, motioning towards the handcuffs.

He lifted his head and smiled. "I don't know. Maybe I should keep you forever as my fiery red-haired sex slave."

"Jake."

He stood up and removed his shirt, exposing his smooth, muscular chest. He tilted his head. "I could fuck you whenever I wanted."

"Jake…"

"Eat you whenever I wanted."

Okay, that made me blush.

He removed his belt buckle and snapped it. "And spank your beautiful ass whenever it was required."

My eyebrows shot up.

He chuckled and dropped the belt. "Or not."

"Please, take these off so that I can touch you," I begged.

"You really don't have much patience, do you?" he said, unbuttoning his jeans.

"Not when I want something this badly," I said, staring at his boxers. I could see a hint of the scar that led underneath the white fabric.

He pushed his boxers down and my eyes widened in pleasure at the size of him. I licked my lips. "Now you *have* to let me touch that."

"Oh, I do, huh?" he said, crawling between my legs.

"Yes." The tip of his penis touched my opening and I spread my legs wider, already anticipating the way he'd fill me. "Please."

He smiled wickedly. "Please what?"

"Release these cuffs or fuck me," I demanded, getting frustrated.

He grabbed the back of my hair and wound it around his hand. "Oh, I like that. Tell me to fuck you again."

"Fuck me."

He pulled my hair tighter and stared into my eyes. "I don't know if I believe that you want it badly enough. Tell me again and this time, make it *believable*."

"Fuck me, Jake. Fuck me hard," I growled.

He raised my thighs and then began to enter me slowly.

"Uh…" I gasped, not having anticipated the actual size of him, even when he'd stood before naked.

"Is this what you wanted?" he whispered huskily as he plunged inside of me.

"Yes," I breathed, feeling him move out and then back in, ever so slowly. Only having been with Scott, I'd never considered anything this dense inside of me.

"You want it harder or faster?"

Oh God.

"Both…" I pleaded.

He picked up speed and I gasped in pleasure as I watched his perfectly sculpted body above me, driving me crazy with every thrust. Then, just when I thought I could actually handle the pressure of his movements, he raised my legs over his shoulders and began driving into me even harder.

"Fuck, you're so tight," he groaned through clenched teeth.

I closed my eyes and moaned as he moved deeper with every movement, creating more pleasure in places I'd never felt before. "Jake, dammit, remove these cuffs," I demanded.

He stopped moving and I sighed in relief as he leaned over and grabbed a set of keys from the nightstand, finally releasing me.

I slid my hands around his neck and kissed him in gratitude as he entered me again. "Yes," I moaned as his hips moved faster and I felt another orgasm beginning to form. Just as I was about to go over the edge, however, he flipped me over like a ragdoll and thrust back inside of me, holding me by the hips this time. Seconds later, my body trembled and quivered and I could feel myself constricting around him as I came.

"Oh, fuck," he groaned. "Lindsey…"

I put my hand over the one he had on my breast and squeezed as he shuddered against me and then quickly pulled out.

"Wouldn't want you to get pregnant," he said, leaning over me.

I smiled. "No worries. I'm on the pill."

His eyes widened and he slapped my ass playfully. "Fuck, you should have told me."

"Sorry."

He pulled me against him and kissed the side of my neck. "Next time, I'm staying inside," he whispered into my ear.

"Next time?"

He smiled, arrogantly. "Of course."

"You're a really confident guy," I teased. "But now I understand why."

"Face it, beautiful, you'll be back for more of this guy," he said, pointing towards his crotch.

I burst out laughing. "You're such a …man."

"Damn right and I'll prove it again if you give me a few minutes to recover."

I touched his thigh. "I think a few minutes is all I have until my mother comes looking for me," I said.

He cringed. "Oh, that's right. Mom is in town. I feel like a teenager again."

"Tell me about it," I said.

Just then his cell phone began to ring. He pulled it out of his jeans and swore.

"Duty calls?" I asked, wrapping a blanket around my nakedness.

He nodded. "Looks like it. I'm going to check in and see what's happening."

"Okay," I said, admiring his chiseled butt as he walked out of the bedroom.

"Be right back!" he called. "Don't move."

I looked at the clock and groaned, it was after midnight and I had too much to do in the morning. As I reached down to grab my clothes, I noticed the drawer to his nightstand was still slightly ajar. I put my hand down to close it when something inside caught my eye. Curiosity got the better of me, and I opened it.

"What the hell?" I whispered, reaching for the stack of photographs. The one on top was of me, lying in my bed, apparently sleeping. As I looked through the other dozen or so photos, my hands began to shake. *All* of the images were of me within the last few days – a couple outside of the gun shop, a few when I was entering the salon with Darcy, and one *somehow* taken when I was in the middle of getting undressed in my bedroom.

I heard the floorboards creak from Jake's footsteps and quickly put the photographs back in the drawer. I wanted to confront him but part of me was so shaken, I was at a loss for words.

"What?" I asked, noticing a look of rage on his face when he entered the room.

"Fuck," he mumbled, running a hand through his hair. "Something came up again on this damn case I'm on and now I have to drive back down to the station."

I stared at him, my heart pounding wildly in my chest, still shocked that he had all of those photos. The thought of him following me around and snapping pictures was a little more than disturbing. "Jake…"

He bent down and grabbed his clothes then started getting dressed. "Damn job – it literally controls my fucking life."

I cleared my throat. "Jake, we really need to talk."

He sat down next to me on the bed. "You know, I'd love more than anything to stay and talk with you, but can it wait until I get back – when there's more time?"

I nodded.

He kissed my lips and then stood up. "Thanks, Lindsey. I really have to get down there before shit hits the fan. I wish I could tell you about it, but I'm not allowed to discuss my cases. You understand?"

I nodded.

He pointed at the blanket wrapped around me and smiled. "You'd better get dressed before you leave. Not that I wouldn't mind having you here, naked and waiting for me when I return."

I picked my clothing up from the floor and began getting dressed.

"You okay?" he asked, combing his hair.

"Yes," I lied. "Why?"

He shrugged. "You're so quiet. You don't regret tonight, do you?"

The truth was, I wasn't so sure. I still couldn't get over the pictures. I had to bite my tongue to avoid going off on a tangent in front of him – I wanted to shout out my frustrations and ask him, why...why the hell was he following me around and taking these pictures? But something kept me from doing it. A nervous voice in my head that told me to wait.

"No," I lied, again.

He kissed the top of my head. "Good, because I'm already hard thinking about the next time."

Chapter Twenty-five

I went back home and tried to sleep but my head was racing with unanswered questions. The more I thought about the pictures, the angrier I became. Not only was it disturbing, but it made me question everything I knew about the man. He kept a strange schedule, went in to work at the most inopportune times, and hadn't even flinched when he'd talked about murdering the men who were terrorizing me. I knew he had to be a cop, but was there something more to him, something dangerous? I decided to keep my distance until my mother took the kids to Florida with her.

Hell, maybe I'd go with them.

Those thoughts finally helped me to fall asleep.

The next day I was kept busy with Scott's funeral arrangements as well as trying to avoid reporters who started calling early and eventually arrived at our doorstep in small groups.

"Knew this was coming," said my mother, peeking through the blinds at the news van parked outside.

I rubbed a hand across my forehead. "I was hoping they'd just call and we could tell them, 'no comment' then hang up."

"The vultures," she replied. "They don't care about the victims. It's all about the story and keeping their ratings up."

I sighed. "At least I kept the kids home. They don't have to talk to anyone about it yet."

My mother turned around and studied me. "You were gone for quite a while last night."

I shrugged. "Just discussing the case with Detective Sharp."

She smiled. "I saw him earlier this morning, he was coming home. He's certainly a good-looking man."

"Can't argue that."

"Is he married?"

"Why, are you interested?" I asked, smiling.

She chuckled. "No, he's much too young for me. I was just curious."

I sighed. "He's *not* married."

Her eyes lit up. "Interesting."

"Why is that interesting?" I asked, although I knew the answer; she was already trying to decide how intimate my relationship with Jake was. Before Scott, I'd dated quite a few guys and there was never much of an interim between them. It had been a little different with Jake, however. I hadn't been looking, it had just happened.

"It just is," she said. "By the way, I'm taking the kids shopping and out for a late lunch. I think they could use a little distraction."

I sighed. "They'll love that. Thank you, mom."

She nodded. "Distractions are nice. Even the living ones."

"What is that supposed to mean?"

"I'm just saying that spending time with a young, handsome cop isn't the worst thing in the world."

I closed my eyes and sighed. "Mom, my husband just died."

"That's true, but he also broke your heart, honey. Quite frankly, he stopped being your husband the moment he dropped his pants for someone else."

"Scott had claimed that he still loved me."

"He may have loved you, but I guarantee he was no longer 'in love' with you. There's a difference. I learned that when your father cheated on me."

That had been over thirty years ago, but a very memorable nightmare. His affair had lasted for six months before my mother had caught on. She'd kicked him out and he'd quickly moved in with the other woman, his secretary. Ten years later, they'd both died in a car crash after returning from an office Christmas party. He'd had too much to drink and had apparently lost control of the vehicle. Although my mother had finally gotten over the ordeal, she still struggled with it once in a while; especially, around the holidays.

"Well, you're probably right," I said.

"So," she said. "Invite that sexy neighbor over for dinner while I'm here, so I can read his aura."

I groaned. "Mom, we're just friends."

"These days you can also have friends with benefits," she said with a wink.

I bit back a smile. "Mom, I have to say, you're unpredictable. I never know what's going to come out of your mouth."

"Life is too short to bite your tongue. I'd rather speak my mind than keep everything bottled up inside. It's something I learned after your father was out of the picture. It's very liberating, you should try it."

I thought about the confrontation with Jerry the other day. "Actually, I'm getting better at speaking my mind, too."

"Good. Keep it up. Now that you're a single mother, you can't afford to let people step all over you."

I took a deep breath and then confided in her about the ordeal with the cop and how someone had broken into the house. I wanted her to know what was happening, to protect her as well as my children.

"You have to call the police," she said, looking horrified.

"Mom, a *cop* is threatening me. One who, apparently, has other family members in the very same profession. Nobody would believe me and it might cause more retaliation. I can't afford to take that chance."

She sighed. "Did you tell your neighbor?"

I nodded. "Yeah, I told Jake and he's helping me with it."

"What is he going to do?" she asked.

"I'm not really sure. I'm hoping he can find some way to threaten them to leave me alone at the very least. All I know is that he promised to help and I hope he can come through."

"But it's still too dangerous. Well, that settles it, then, you're moving in with me; at least until it's safe."

"Actually, I would like the children to leave with you, as soon as the funeral is over. I have to stick around. "

Her eyes narrowed. "You're coming, too. Don't be silly."

I raised my hands. "Mom, I need to stay here."

"No you don't."

We argued about it for a while until I agreed to think about it.

She walked over to me and put her arm around my shoulders. "You'll get through this, honey. I'm here for you now and whatever I can do, don't hesitate to ask."

I smiled weakly. "Thanks, mom."

She nodded. "Let me know if you invite the neighbor, though, so I don't leave my reefer sitting out."

I groaned. "Mom, you actually brought the marijuana?"

She nodded. "Of course; it helps my Rheumatoid Arthritis, dear."

"Right."

Her eyes widened. "Oh, believe what you want, but it's the truth."

"Well, don't let Regan or Jeremy see it."

She shrugged. "Too late now, we smoked a bowl together last night."

"Mom!"

She threw her head back and laughed. "You're so gullible."

As I pretended to swat her, my cell phone began to ring.

Jake.

"Hi," I said.

"Hi, Lindsey. Listen," he sighed. "I have to leave town."

My eyes widened. "What?"

"It's this case, again. My informant skipped town last night and its imperative that we track him down before someone else does. Anyway, I'll be back in a couple of days."

"I understand."

"By the way, I've hired someone to keep an eye on you; a friend of mine."

"Who?"

"You probably won't even know he's around. His name is Carter and he's going to make sure nobody fucks with you."

"But…"

"I don't have much time. Carter knows that your life is in danger, but that's about it. I haven't told him anything else."

I walked over to the window and looked outside. Besides the news van, nobody else was around. "Where is he?"

"He won't be out in the open, but believe me, he's around."

I closed the blinds. "Well, thanks."

"No problem. I don't want anything happening to you when I'm away. If something should go wrong, though, you call me immediately."

"Okay."

He lowered his voice. "Lindsey, last night was…amazing, and I know we've only known each other for a short time, but fuck if I can't stop thinking about you."

I thought about the photos again. "Jake, I have to ask you –"

"Yeah, I'll be right there!" he hollered, his mouth away from the phone.

I hesitated. "Jake."

"Shit, Lindsey, I have to go. I'll call you tonight."

I sighed. "Sure."

After he hung up, I went around the house and looked through all of the windows, curious as to where Carter would be hiding. It was a relief but also a little unnerving to know that we were being watched. Not finding any traces of him, however, I gave up and began calling the rest of our friends to let them know about Scott.

Chapter Twenty-Six

"Are you sure you don't want to come with us, honey?" asked my mother, two hours later.

"No," I said. "I'm going to go through our bills and see where we really do stand financially."

"Knowing Scott, he probably had some kind of life insurance policy. You should check with his employer."

I nodded. "I will."

My mom looked past me. "Oh, here they come. Ready to go, kiddos?"

"Yes, grandma," said Regan, looking pale. She had her hair pulled severely into a ponytail which emphasized the new circles under her eyes.

"Are you okay?" I asked, moving towards her.

"Peachy," she mumbled, blinking back tears.

I pulled her into my arms. "I know, it really sucks."

"Do you think we'll get interviewed coming out of the house?" asked Jeremy, looking through the living room window at the reporter walking up and down the sidewalk, smoking a cigarette and talking on the phone.

"No," I said, releasing Regan. "And if any of them do bother you, tell them 'no comment.'"

"But I *want* to be on television," he said.

"Not for this," I said.

"Fine," he huffed.

"Quit being such a dork," said Regan.

He glared at his sister. "You're the dork, not me."

"No fighting," scolded my mother. "Or I won't buy you anything at the mall."

"That reminds me, don't go overboard, mom," I said.

She sniffed. "Nonsense. I don't get to visit my grandkids that often and today I'm going to make up for it."

Regan's face lit up and that alone was worth the extra gifts from my mom.

"Fine," I said. "Just remember, however, that Christmas is coming. If you buy them too much today, their Christmas list will probably dwindle down to nothing."

"Right," snorted Regan.

She waved her hand. "Don't worry, Lindsey. I know what I'm doing."

I crossed my arms. "I hope so."

Ten minutes later they were gone and I took on the task of trying to find out how bad our financial problems really were. After looking through our credit card bills and making some phone calls to our mortgage company, I wanted to join Scott. We were several months late on our mortgage, and were on the verge of being foreclosed on.

We were in dire straits.

"I don't understand," I said. "We haven't been receiving anything in the mail. I haven't seen any statements or late notices."

"Your husband has online statements set up; however, we have sent several letters to your home regarding the missed payments," replied the woman.

I rubbed my forehead. "Well, my husband just passed away, and at this point, I'm not sure when I can even make a payment," I said.

"I'm sorry for your loss, Mrs. Shepard. I hope you don't mind my asking, but did your husband have a life insurance policy? That might help your situation."

"I guess I'll have to find that out," I said.

I hung up with the mortgage company and called Scott's employer.

"I'm so sorry for your loss," said Dave from Human Resources. "He was a really nice guy."

"Thank you," I said, blinking back tears. I'd met Dave at one of the Christmas parties and remembered how he and Scott had joked around together.

"Well," he said, clearing his throat. "It looks like he did have a life insurance policy."

"Oh, thank God," I said. "I spoke to our mortgage company earlier, and I guess we owe a lot of money."

"It looks like you should be able to catch up," he said. "Considering his policy is for two million dollars."

I opened my mouth but nothing came out.

"Mrs. Shepard?"

"What did you say?" I whispered.

"His life insurance policy is for two million dollars. I'll try and rush the paperwork to you so that you can send it in to the insurance company. Due to the nature of his death, however, it might take a while for them to release that kind of money."

"I… understand," I said, still stunned that Scott had taken out such a large insurance policy. "I just had no idea that he would have taken out such a big policy."

Dave sighed. "If its one thing I knew about your husband, it was that he loved you and the kids. He wanted to make sure you were provided for in the event of his death."

I swallowed back the lump in my throat.

"So," he continued. "I'll mail this out to you as soon as possible."

"Thank you, Dave."

After hanging up, I sat down in the kitchen and put my head in my hands. While I was relieved that our financial problems would be taken care of, the fact that Scott was gone seemed more real than ever.

I spent the rest of the day looking through old photo albums, trying to bring back better memories. Unfortunately, it made things worse. By the time I'd made it through the first album, the one showing our wedding, I was a wreck.

I pushed the albums aside and decided to take a shower before my mom arrived back with the kids. When I finished, I put my robe on and stepped back into my bedroom. It was then that I noticed my mother had left a message for me to call her.

"What's going on?" I asked.

"Oh, this rental car," she huffed. "One of the tires is completely flat. We're at the mall, waiting for the rental company to bring me out a new car."

"Would you like me to pick up the kids?" I asked.

"No," she replied. "As soon as they make the switch, I'm taking them to a movie. We're going to that new *Batman* movie."

I smiled; it must have been Jeremy's idea. "Okay."

"Would you like to meet us?"

"No thanks, mom. Have fun."

"I will. Even grandmothers can appreciate a tight-fitting costume like Batman's."

"I'm sure," I said.

"Well, we'll see you later."

"Oh, I almost forgot. Molly and Henry wanted to take the kids overnight."

"Okay," she said. "With that in mind, we'll come home right after the movie so the kids can each pack an overnight bag. Then I'll drive them over myself. I haven't seen Molly since Caroline's wedding and should pay my respects."

"Thanks, mom."

"No problem at all."

I hung up and slipped on a T-shirt and a pair of sweats. Then, I made myself a glass of iced coffee and sat down on the porch with my Kindle. As I took a sip, I noticed a car pull up to Jake's house. I watched as a tall blonde got out of her car. She wore a tight black skirt and a blue short-sleeved blouse that showed off her perfect, model-like body. She walked up to Jake's door and began knocking. After getting no response, she stormed back to her car with an angry scowl on her face.

I took another drink of my coffee just as she noticed me on the porch. When she moved away from her car and towards my house, I groaned inwardly, wondering what in the hell she wanted.

"Excuse me!" she called, raising her hand in greeting.

"Yes?" I asked as she stopped at the bottom of the steps.

"Would you happen to know if your neighbor has been home recently?"

I cleared my throat. "Well, he was home last night."

"Hmm…I wonder if I should wait around for him," she mumbled, turning to look back at his house.

"I think he may have gone out of town," I said. "For some case he's working on."

She raised her eyebrows. "A case?"

I nodded.

"He actually told you he was working on 'a case'?" she asked.

"Why, is that strange?" I asked.

She snorted. "Because he hasn't been working for the past few months and owes me a lot of money. At least that's what he told me. No wonder he's been avoiding my phone calls."

I straightened up. "Really?"

She folded her arms under her chest. "Yeah. Apparently he's forgotten that he has a five-year-old son who needs food and clothing."

"He has a son?" I asked, stunned.

She nodded. "That's right. If you see him, tell him his ex, Connie, stopped by and I'm royally fucking pissed. If he wants to see Michael anymore, he'd better pay up. My job doesn't cover all of our son's expenses."

I swallowed the lump in my throat. "So, you're his ex-wife?"

She smiled bitterly. "Well, *almost* ex. He refuses to sign the paperwork. I've tried divorcing the bastard several times, but he doesn't like giving up his 'possessions', I guess."

I stared at her in astonishment as she turned and stomped away.

Chapter Twenty-seven

When the initial shock finally wore off, I went into the house and called Jake's cell phone, pissed as all hell, but of course, he didn't answer. I had a feeling he'd already gotten another voicemail from Connie after our conversation, and was now avoiding me. Whatever kind of game he was playing, I really wanted no part of.

Needing someone who'd listen to my rants willingly, I tried calling Darcy, but she didn't answer. I left her a message to call me back as soon as possible.

Feeling completely vexed about everything happening in my life, I paced around the house for the next couple of hours, trying to make sense of it all. When Darcy hadn't returned my calls and the sun started going down, I grabbed my keys and decided to go for a drive. I left the house without having any kind of destination in mind. I just wanted to get away from everything and clear my mind.

Not an easy task.

By the time I made it halfway through town, I was fuming again and had to force myself not to call Jake's cell phone and let him have it. Instead, I tried Darcy once again, but there still was still no answer. It was now beginning to worry me; it *never* took her this long to call me back.

Sighing, I turned my SUV towards her apartment and was relieved when I noticed her car in the parking lot.

I shut off my engine and went inside to try and buzz her apartment, but she didn't respond. Fortunately, her friendly neighbor from across the hall let me in as she was walking out.

I took the elevator up to Darcy's and knocked on the door several times. I could hear her stereo playing, but as many times as I knocked, she still wouldn't answer.

"Darcy?" I called. "It's Linds, open up!"

After several attempts, I turned the knob and found that it was unlocked. I swung the door open and poked my head through. "Darcy?"

No answer.

Her apartment was dark as I entered. I shut the door behind me and turned on the hallway light.

"Max?" I hollered.

Still not getting a response from anyone, I walked into her family room, but found it empty. I then turned and went to search her bedroom. The door was closed when I approached it.

"Darcy?" I asked, knocking loudly. "It's me."

No answer.

Worried and not caring anymore if I was about to interrupt some kind of passionate interlude, I opened the door and found the light on.

"Hello?" I called, peeking into her bedroom. When I noticed the stacks of clothing on her mattress, I sighed in relief.

She must be doing laundry somewhere in the building.

As I was about to turn and walk away, I noticed the door to her private bathroom was closed and the mauve carpet surrounding it was sopping wet. The hair on the back of my neck stood straight up as I walked towards the door.

"Darcy?" I called, knocking on the door.

No answer but I could definitely hear water running from inside.

Alarmed, I knocked harder. "Darcy, are you okay?!"

Still not getting any kind of answer, I turned the knob and stepped inside.

"No!" I gasped, rushing towards her bathtub. "Oh, my God!"

The oversized porcelain tub was overflowing with water and looking up at me with vacant eyes, was my very best friend.

"Darcy!" I choked.

Someone had placed a large, metal barbell over her neck to hold her down and her hands were cuffed in front of her pale, naked body.

Crying, I tried lifting the barbell, but it was much too heavy. Feeling helpless, I stood up and backed away, realizing in horror that she'd obviously been murdered.

Sobbing hysterically, I grabbed my cell phone and called nine-one-one.

"Stay calm, ma'am," said the operator. Someone should be there shortly.

"Okay," I hiccupped.

By the time the police arrived, I'd stopped crying but was still in shock. My husband had been murdered and now my dearest friend.

Oh God, poor Max!

He adored his mother and would be totally devastated. My heart ached for the little boy who had been trying to adjust to his parents' divorce and now had to live without the love of his mother. I felt like I was in a living nightmare that kept growing and claiming new victims.

After the police took my statement, I called my mother and left her a message to call me back. As I hung up, the detectives working on Scott's case stepped through the door.

"Mrs. Shepard," murmured Parker, with a grim expression. "I'd hoped to never meet with you under similar circumstances. I'm terribly sorry to hear about your friend."

I nodded and wiped my face. "I know. I just don't understand what's going on."

Franklin's eyes narrowed. "Well, it's probably safe to say that these two deaths are related. I think we need to sit down again and try to figure out what the hell is going on."

"I know," I sniffed. "My best friend and husband have been murdered, my kids threatened. I just don't know how much more of this I can take."

Parker raised his eyebrows. "Your kids were threatened?"

Crap.

I sighed. "Yes. I guess we need to talk about that, too."

The two cops looked at each other and then turned back to me.

"You have something to tell us?" asked Parker.

"I don't know for certain but I think I might have an idea of who's behind these murders," I said.

Chapter Twenty-eight

I sat down with the two detectives and started from the beginning, telling them about my first encounter with Tina, the confrontation with Jerry, and getting threatened by an unknown assailant. The only thing I left out was Jake's involvement.

"So, someone broke into your home and threatened you, and that was *before* your husband was murdered?" said Parker.

I crossed my arms under my chest. "I was frightened. The man threatened the lives of my children."

"You should have called the police," said Franklin with a disapproving look. "Now two people are dead."

I sighed. "But Jerry is a cop and I believe the man who threatened me is, too."

"Do you know this *Jerry's* last name?" asked Parker, writing in his notepad.

"Actually, I guess I don't," I said. "I know he's a cop only because I saw him in uniform."

"You have the address for him and his wife, Tina?" asked Franklin.

I told them the street and a description of the townhome. "It's the one for sale. You know, I'm not even sure if they're still living there. In fact, I heard that he might be staying in the hospital right now. That he recently had surgery."

"Really?" asked Parker. "So, he'd probably have an alibi tonight, if that's the case."

I nodded. "Probably, but he has someone else doing his dirty work for him, anyway."

"We'll try and locate Jerry and his wife," said Franklin.

I frowned. "What if his goon comes after me or my kids? Now that I've reported it to you guys, we're sitting ducks."

Parker scratched his head. "We'll get you some protection. I'll appoint a couple of officers to watch over your family for the next couple of weeks or until we crack this case."

I sighed. "Thank you."

"Is there anything else you'd like to add?" asked Franklin.

"Well, Darcy told me that she had a date tomorrow night," I said. "Some guy she met on an online dating site."

Parker nodded and scratched his dark blonde stubbly chin. "Interesting. Do you know which site she used?"

I shook my head. "No."

"Well, we'll be going through her computer and files to see if there's anything that might help locate her killer. I'm sure we'll figure out the dating site as well."

"By the way," I said. "Did you talk to those women I told you about? The ones my husband was messing around with?"

Franklin nodded. "Yes, and they both have alibis for the night your husband was murdered."

"Figures," I said.

Parker sighed. "Interestingly enough, they don't deny the sexual relationship one bit. The two women live together and own a pretty successful shoe business. It appears that your husband was working on some new advertising gimmick for them."

"It wasn't all he was working on," I said, looking down at my wedding ring, wondering why I hadn't yet removed it.

"The women were definitely on their own agenda," said Franklin. "At first glance, you'd take them for a couple of straight-laced gals, but once we started asking questions, they pretty much boasted about their sexual exploits. They're a little strange, but you can't arrest them for that."

"Bummer," I said.

"Are you sure that's all you have for us?" asked Parker.

I sighed. "I don't know. If there is anything else, I'll call you."

"Good. Now, I'm going to make a couple of phone calls so you'll have someone watching your house. Meanwhile, keep the rest of your family in tow," said Parker.

"You mentioned phone calls earlier. I'm going to have your phone tapped, just in case it brings us any leads," said Franklin.

I raised my cell phone. "Speaking of phone calls, I still have one of the numbers in my cell phone; the number of the woman who called and eventually texted me."

"Could you find that for us?" asked Parker.

I scrolled through my call history until I reached the number in question. "This is the only one that doesn't pop up as a 'private' number," I said.

Parker took the phone from me. "This might be a break. As far as the unlisted numbers, we can get that information from the phone company."

"So, um…are you going to call that number?" I asked as he wrote it down.

Parker shook his head. "Not yet. I want to put a trace on the number and see whose it is before I even think about calling them. If they're connected to these murders, they might bolt if we don't do this right."

"Chances are they dumped that number anyway," said Franklin. "They'd have to be complete idiots to kill someone and leave their phone number out there for us to find."

"I'm almost positive it was Jerry's wife, Tina," I said.

"Well, leave it to us. We'll check out this Jerry character and see if we can come up with something," said Franklin.

"Mrs. Shepard, this isn't an easy question to ask, but I have to do it," said Parker.

I sighed. "No, I did not kill my best friend, Detective."

"Thanks for that, although it isn't the question I had in mind. My question is, did Darcy and Scott have any kind of sexual relationship?"

I stared at him in horror. "No. Darcy was my best friend!" I paused, feeling my eyes fill up with tears. "She would *never* do something like that."

"Was there anyone else she may have had a sexual relationship with?" asked Franklin.

I smiled bitterly. "No. She was pretty loyal to Herbie, actually."

Parker's eyebrows shot up. "Herbie?"

I wiped away another tear and smiled bitterly. "Forget it, private joke."

Chapter Twenty-nine

"Mom," I said into my cell phone twenty minutes later as I sat in Darcy's parking lot. "Where *are* you?"

"We just got home. My cell phone died, I'm sorry I missed your call, dear. What's going on?"

I swallowed the lump in my throat. "It's Darcy," I squeaked. "She's been murdered."

There was a sharp intake of breath and then she moaned. "No! Darcy? How? Why?"

"I don't know, exactly," I sniffed, cradling the phone on my shoulder while I reached for a tissue. "It might be related to Scott's death."

"For the love of God, Lindsey! You need to go the police or the FBI. This isn't something you can just run and hide from."

I sighed. "I know. I spoke to the detectives on Scott's case and they know about it now. Which reminds me, we'll be under surveillance for a while by the police, to make sure we're protected."

"What about Jake's guy?"

I snorted. "I doubt Jake really had a guy watching out for us."

"Why do you say that?"

"Because, I've caught him in a couple of lies so I don't really believe anything he's told me."

"Really? He seemed like such a nice man, too. He even stopped by when we arrived home from the movie tonight." she said.

My throat went dry. "What?"

Jake was back?

"Yes. He was looking for you. I didn't know exactly where you were and he seemed quite agitated when I told him that."

"Well, he has my number, too," I said.

"He told me that someone stole his cell phone and that he didn't know your number by heart yet."

Right.

"Well, I'll be home, soon. I have a few things to say to him, actually."

"Poor Darcy," sighed my mother. "I just can't believe it. First Scott and now her? I'm really frightened, Lindsey."

"It'll be okay," I told her, although I was quite scared myself.

"Oh, somebody's at the door. I'll see you in a little while."

"Wait, mom! Don't…"

Click.

I sighed as the phone went dead. "Crap," I mumbled, tossing my phone onto the passenger seat. Now that things were getting much more dangerous, I didn't want her just answering the door for anyone. But knowing my mother, she'd throw the door open and invite the person in with a friendly smile.

When I reached my house, I noticed that Jake's lights were on. Part of me was happy that I'd get the chance to have it out with him; the other was somewhat scared of the actual confrontation. I'd always avoided conflict until I was forced to face it and even now I debated on just simply giving him the cold shoulder.

Sighing, I pulled into my driveway and got out of the SUV. As I walked up the steps, my front door swung open.

I stared in surprise. "Lieutenant Parker – what are you doing here?"

He smiled. "I couldn't find anyone to cover your place for the next couple of hours, so I decided to do it myself until backup came. So for now, you're stuck with me."

I moved past him into my house. "Well, thank you for that. Where's Franklin?"

He shut the door. "We'd driven separately to Darcy's tonight because he had to get home to his kids."

I cocked my ear. The house seemed unusually quiet for eight-thirty. "That's fine, he infuriates me anyway. So, where are my mom and the kids?" I asked, setting my purse down.

"Oh, they're fine. Kids are up in their rooms and your mom is lying down. She mentioned that she had a long day."

Something about the way he watched me was a little unnerving. If I didn't know it, I'd say he was actually checking me out. I cleared my throat. "Okay. Well, would you like some coffee?"

He stepped closer and pulled a piece of lint from the front of my T-shirt, near my right nipple, as I held my breath. "Sure," he said, smiling. "But only if you'll join me."

"Sure," I answered, quickly, turning around and leading him towards the kitchen. "You know, I have one of those Keurigs. I can make a cup in less than two minutes."

"That sounds great then."

"Sit down, please," I said, motioning towards the counter stools.

"That's okay. I need to stretch my legs out a little. You don't mind?"

"No, not at all. So, um, do you have any kids?" I asked.

He smiled. "No. Not with my job."

"I'm sure you're always working."

"Yeah. Plus, I have a pretty big family. If I want to see kids, I just go visit one of my nephews."

"That's good. Are you married?" I asked, trying to keep up the small talk.

His lips thinned. "No."

Although I'd noticed he looked perpetually tired, he was still very a good-looking man, so I assumed he had girlfriends. "Well, marriage is tough," I said. "You're probably better off not being married, especially with your busy career."

"Well, it's not only that," he said moving closer to me.

Too close, actually.

An alarm went off in my head and I took a step back until my buttocks touched the counter. "Oh?"

He closed the distance, trapping me. "I'd fucking kill myself if I had one of you whores waiting for me at home," he growled.

I felt like he'd sucked all the air out of my body. I couldn't breathe. Instead, I just stared at him in horror.

An evil grin spread across his face. "Figured it out yet?"

"I…"

He grabbed my right breast and squeezed it painfully. "Does this help? It's not the first time I've touched your tits."

"No!" I cried out, pushing against him, but he was strong.

He grabbed the back of my hair with one hand and my throat with the other. "Now listen here, you stupid bitch," he spat. "We're going for a little ride. You come, without a fight, and I won't kill your fucking mom or your pain-in-the-ass kids."

"They're alive?" I whispered.

His eyes penetrated mine. "For now. You come with me peacefully and they'll stay that way. Otherwise, I'll skin them alive, right in front of you."

Realizing he'd probably killed Scott and Darcy, I knew his threats were more than valid.

I let out a whimper and nodded.

"Good," he said, loosening his hold on my neck. "Don't you dare try and fuck with me, though. I'll make sure you regret it for the rest of your life."

I shook my head. "I won't."

Just then, someone rang the doorbell.

"Fuck, who the hell is that, now?" he snapped.

"I don't know," I replied in a shaky voice. "The cops?"

He paused for a minute and shook his head. "No. I don't think so. Get rid of whoever it is," he ordered, pushing me out of the kitchen. "Tell them you're in mourning or something," he said following me. "Say what you have to say to make them leave or I'll kill everyone in this house."

The doorbell rang a second time as we moved towards the front door. He pulled out his gun and stood to the side of it. "Open it," he whispered.

I cleared my throat and opened the door.

"Jesus, Lindsey," exclaimed Jake, his hands on his hips. "What the hell is going on?"

"I'm… just… tired," I murmured, trying to remain calm. "It's been a really, long day."

His studied me. "Are you okay?"

I forced a smile. "Yes. I'm fine. Like I said, just had a long day."

His eyes narrowed for a fraction of a second and then returned to normal. "I understand," he said. "The funeral was today?"

I nodded quickly. "Yeah. I really need to lie down now, Jake. I'll talk to you tomorrow?"

"No problem. I'll see you soon. Sleep well," he answered, turning away.

I stared at him longingly as he stepped off the porch. Even after everything he'd done, I knew that Jake was saner than the person standing next to me, aiming a gun at my head.

"Close the fucking door," whispered Parker.

Trembling, I obeyed.

"Jesus Christ. He's just as stupid as you, even for a cop. A funeral? The body hasn't even been released yet."

My eyes filled with more frustrated tears. To him Scott was just a body, nothing more.

He grabbed my arm and pulled me towards the kitchen and the back of the house.

"Please," I whispered. "I'll do anything you want if you stop this. Please."

He yanked on my arm harder. "Guess what? You're going to do exactly what I want anyway. Just shut the fuck up before I kill you right away so I don't have to listen to your whiny voice one more minute."

"Why are you doing this?" I choked. "I haven't done *anything* to you."

He pushed me against the back door and put the gun to my face. "You're right about that, you didn't do anything to me, but you fucked with my brother, Jerry. I'd do anything to protect him. Kill *anyone* who messes with him."

"Jerry is your brother?"

He smiled, cruelly. "What, you don't see the resemblance?"

I shook my head.

He traced the gun along my cheek. "We had separate fathers," he said with a psychotic gleam in his eyes. "No big deal. Our mother was a fucking whore, just like the rest of you sluts. A good-for-nothing slut who sold herself out and never protected either of us when we really needed it. But

I won't let my brother down. Nobody will ever *fuck* with him again, not if I can help it."

"But…"

His face twisted into a scowl. "No more questions. Let's get out of here and have us a little fun." He then pulled me away from the door and opened it.

"Just one more question, did you really kill Scott and Darcy?" I whispered.

He grabbed my arm and pulled me outside. "Wouldn't you like to know."

"Please," I begged. "Just tell me."

He stopped and turned to face me. The satisfied grin on his face made me recoil in horror. "Let's just say…"

Before he could finish, a large shadow rushed Parker from the side, tackling him to the ground. I quickly moved away from the two struggling men, and back into the house.

I slammed the door and locked it. "Ohmygod," I sobbed.

A gunshot went off, and it was at that point I'd remembered my own revolver. I rushed to the bedroom to grab the gun from my closet when I heard someone kick the back door down.

Terrified, I raised the gun and pointed it towards my bedroom door, my hands shaking as I waited.

Crap, the safety!

I unlocked it and pointed the gun towards the door just as it was flung open. Frightened beyond belief, I pulled the trigger and fired.

"Lindsey!" grunted Jake, falling down to his knees.

"No!" I choked, rushing towards him as he collapsed to the floor. I bent down on my knees and touched his flushed face. "Jake, oh, my God – are you okay?"

He groaned. "I…"

It was then that I heard the click of a gun and looked up to find Parker aiming his towards my head.

He smiled triumphantly. "Looks like you shot lover boy by mistake. How unfortunate for you."

I stared at him incredulously. "I thought…"

He snorted. "What, that he'd killed me?"

I didn't answer.

"Let's go, Lindsey," he demanded. "Hand me your gun first."

"It's there," I said, pointing towards the floor.

He reached out his hand. "Fine, bring it to me, and no funny business."

I glanced at Jake's still form and swallowed the lump in my throat.

"Get the fucking gun now!"

I nodded and crawled towards the revolver, grabbing it.

"Bring it to me," he ordered.

Before I could move, Jake's arms snaked out and grabbed Parker's ankles, making him lose his balance. Parker screamed in rage as he fell forward. Then, at the last minute, he twisted his body and aimed his revolver at Jake's head.

But, I fired my gun first.

The bullet caught Parker in the cheek and I watched in horror as his face became a grisly mess of cartilage and blood.

"Oh God!" I shuddered, closing my eyes.

"You okay?" asked Jake, crawling towards me.

I dropped my gun, now shaking uncontrollably. I nodded and wiped my face.

"Lindsey," he whispered, standing up.

"I…I don't understand," I asked, incredulously. "How come you're not dead?"

He smiled, grimly. "I'm wearing a bulletproof vest."

"How did you know?"

"I knew there was something wrong right away," he said, pulling me up and into his arms.

I pushed him away. "I have to go check on my family."

"Of course."

He followed me as I rushed out of the room and ran up the upstairs.

"Thank God!" I cried, never feeling so relieved in my life. Tied to three of my folding chairs were my mother and two children, very much alive but obviously terrified beyond belief. I removed the duct tape from my mother's mouth while Jake began freeing the children.

"Did you catch that bastard?" hollered my mother.

I kneeled down to free her feet. "Yes. He's gone. Are you guys okay?" I asked noticing the bruise on her face.

"I'm fine," said my mother. "So are the kids."

Regan wiped her tears and nodded. "Is he really gone?"

I stood up and pulled Regan into my arms while Jake freed Jeremy. "Yes, honey."

"He said he'd kill you if we tried to escape," sobbed Jeremy.

"He's gone, honey," I said. "He can't hurt anyone."

"I'll call the police," said Jake, standing back up.

"Thank you," I said, now holding both of my kids tightly.

"Who was he?" asked my mother, rubbing her wrist. "I didn't even get a chance to see his face. He wore a mask."

I told her everything I knew while Jake walked back into the bedroom and listened in.

"I'm so glad I made it back into town," he said after I finished. "I almost missed my flight."

"I thought you were supposed to be gone for a couple of days," I said.

He sighed. "I was misled to believe that my informant had skipped town, and then to top it all off, somebody stole my cell phone. I have a feeling that this Parker character was responsible for that, too. I think he wanted me out of town so he could get to you."

I stared at him for a minute and then turned to my mother. "Watch the kids. I need to talk to Jake alone for a minute."

She nodded. "Of course, dear."

"What's up?" he asked, following me downstairs.

I turned around to face him. "I know."

He raised his eyebrows. "You know?"

I glared at him. "The photos, the lies, your little boy!"

Jake took a step backwards. "My what?"

I laughed coldly. "Your *son*. I met Connie."

"Connie?"

"Don't play me for a fool, Jake. I met your wife!"

He stared at me blankly for a minute and then started laughing.

"Oh, you find this funny?"

He moved towards me, still shaking his head in amusement. "Lindsey…"

I stared at him incredulously. "How dare you laugh!" I snapped.

"Lindsey," he said, grabbing both of my wrists and pulling me towards him. "Just settle down."

I struggled to break free, furious. "Jake, dammit, let me go!"

He tightened his grip. "Lindsey, listen to me, Connie is not my wife, she's married to the guy I'm renting the house from."

I froze and stared up at him. "What?"

He chuckled. "Yes. His name is Tony Bradley and I'm renting the house. Actually, his mother purchased it for him after he and his wife separated. Now he's renting it out to make some extra cash, I guess."

I raised my chin defiantly. "Okay, what about those pictures you have of me in your nightstand? What in the hell is that all about?"

Jake closed his eyes and sighed. "Fuck. I was going to tell you about those photos in time…"

"Is that so?"

He nodded. "Yes. Tina gave those photos to me. She found them in the trunk of Jerry's car and was pissed as all hell."

My eyes widened. "Jerry took them?"

"Either Jerry or Parker. I didn't tell you right away because I knew you were terrified out of your mind already."

I released a long sigh and then looked up at him. "I'm sorry."

He pulled me back into his arms. "No, *I'm* sorry. I should have told you."

"It would have saved me a lot of stress and worry," I said.

"You're right. I was just trying to protect you, though. I guess it backfired."

"Speaking of protection, what ever happened to Carter?"

Jake's face fell. "He's dead, too. I found him in your flower garden when I went through the backyard. Apparently, Parker took him out."

I rested my cheek against his chest. "I'm sorry. Jesus, what a nightmare, huh?"

"At least it's over, though," he said into my hair. "And I didn't lose you."

"But I still lost Darcy," I whispered. "Scott was one thing…but Darcy, we were like sisters."

"Hey," he said, tilting my chin up towards his face. "I bet your friend wouldn't want you dwelling on her death. In fact, wherever she is, she's probably satisfied that you took care of her killer personally."

My lips trembled. "Maybe, but it's still hard to accept that she's gone."

"I know," he said. "But you don't have to face her death alone. I won't let you."

I fell against him and closed my eyes.

Chapter Thirty

One Year Later
Lutsen, Minnesota

"What do you think?"

I looked around the cozy cabin and smiled. "Jake, its perfect."

His eyes sparkled. "Wait until we go skiing. There's nothing like the freedom of flying down the mountain on skis, especially after a fresh coating of snow."

I laughed as I removed my jacket. "The only hill I'm flying down is the one with all the children. I've only been skiing once and it was years ago."

"Oh, you'll graduate off that hill in no time, and then I'll take you down some of the tamer ones."

"Look at you," I said, moving towards him. "I haven't seen you this excited…ever."

He pulled me into his arms. "What's not to be excited about? It's our honeymoon and I have you alone for a full week, without kids or the station interrupting us. I'm ecstatic."

Feeling his excitement pressed up against my stomach I giggled. "Wow, I can tell."

He released me and removed his jacket. "I think we should hit the slopes before it gets dark and then I'm going to wine you, dine you, and then handcuff you to the bed for the rest of the night."

My eyes narrowed. "I told you to leave those at home."

He chuckled. "Still despise the cuffs, huh?"

"I just don't like feeling powerless. I'd rather keep my hands free for other things."

"On that note," he said, slapping my butt, "I'm going to grab the rest of our suitcases so we can start skiing. The faster we get that over with, the faster you can show me what you can do with those hands."

I laughed. "I like that idea, Detective. Meanwhile, I'll go get changed."

An hour later, I stood on the Bunny Hill with three young children, re-learning how to snowplow while Jake went on to tackle the moguls. Fortunately, it didn't take long to graduate to the "easy slopes", and by the time we reunited an hour and a half later, I couldn't wipe the smile from my face.

"Having fun?" he asked, removing his goggles.

I nodded. "I forgot how fun skiing can be."

"It's a blast, isn't it? So, how about a break? Care to join me for a hot drink in the chalet?"

"Sounds good."

The chalet was busy but we lucked out and found an open table by the fireplace. Once seated, I stretched out my legs and let out a satisfied sigh. "This is wonderful, isn't it?"

He grabbed my hand and squeezed it. "I couldn't think of anywhere else I'd rather be than alone with you. I'm a very happy man."

I licked my lips. "Jake, there's something I have to tell you."

He straightened up. "This sounds serious."

"It is."

"Lay it on me."

I smiled. "I'm pregnant."

Expecting him to be as excited as I was, I stared in surprise as his face fell.

"You're what?" he asked.

I leaned forward. "Pregnant. I'm about six weeks. I know I should have told you, but I didn't want you to cancel the trip."

He released my hand. "Are you supposed to be skiing when you're pregnant?" he asked tightly.

I tilted my head and studied him. He looked far from thrilled. "Well, I've been very careful and obviously, I'm not going down anything I can't handle."

He turned and stared at the fire without saying anything.

"What's wrong?" I asked. "I thought you'd be as happy as I am."

He turned back towards me, and for a minute, a spark of anger flashed through his eyes. "Sure, I'm happy," he said.

I narrowed my eyes. "Well, you don't look very happy."

He scowled. "Would you prefer if I jumped up and down, shouting out to the world that my wife got herself pregnant without consulting me first?"

I stared at him in shock. "Excuse me?"

The couple at the next table glanced over at us and he shot them a threatening look. He then turned back to me. "I thought you were done having kids. You already have two," he whispered, angrily.

My jaw dropped. "Jake? What's gotten in to you?" I'd never seen this side of him.

"You told me that you were on the pill."

I nodded. "Yes, but there's always a chance of getting pregnant, even on the pill."

We stared at each other in silence for a few seconds and then he smiled. "Sorry. I just wasn't prepared for that. Of course, I'm happy. It's great news."

The smile still hadn't reached his eyes, which worried me.

"You're sure?" I asked.

He shrugged. "Well, what's done is done. There's nothing we can do about it now."

Wanting to throttle him, I stood up. "This conversation is getting shittier by the minute. I'm going back to the cabin; I'm feeling nauseous all of a sudden."

He pointed at my stomach. "See, another drawback of pregnancy."

I glared at him. "No, *your* attitude is making me sick."

"Lindsey…"

"Leave me alone, Jake," I said, grabbing my jacket.

"You're being silly."

"Oh really? I just told you that you're going to be a father, and from your reaction, it appears that you'd rather shoot yourself in the head. I guess I still don't know what kind of a man you really are, Detective," I spat.

He didn't respond, which made it even worse. Scowling, I turned and stormed out of the chalet, ignoring the curious stares of the people sitting near our table.

***

Back in the cabin, I took a hot shower and slipped on an oversized sweater and leggings. Still fuming about Jake's reaction, I grabbed my Kindle and tried forgetting about it, but it wasn't easy.

"Dammit," I muttered, slamming the thing against the cushion of the leather sofa.

I still couldn't believe Jake's reaction. I'd expected the same kind of joy I'd felt when seeing the plus sign on the test strip. But his reaction appeared to be of disgust, which confused the hell out of me. He'd seemed so loving towards *my* kids that I'd only assumed he'd want one of his own.

Frustrated, I turned on the television and began flipping through the channels, waiting for Jake to return. We definitely needed to talk about his attitude before our child was born. There was no way I'd raise a baby around someone who wasn't interested in children. If that meant leaving him, well then, so be it.

Two hours later, after getting caught up in an 'Oprah' marathon on cable, I fell into a troubled sleep.

Chapter Thirty-one

Something was vibrating.

I opened my eyes and looked at the clock. It was almost midnight and Jake hadn't yet made it back to the cabin.

Sighing, I sat up and stretched my arms as one of Jake's suitcases began vibrating. I unzipped it and found a cell phone inside of a brown leather jacket; a phone I didn't recognize. It was an older flip phone, and when I opened it, I noticed there was a new picture-mail, sent by a number I did recognize.

Jake's.

Curious as to why he'd be sending a photo to this particular phone, I opened up the message and stared at it in shock.

"What the hell?"

It was a photo of a naked woman, lying in the snow, her lifeless eyes staring past the camera, bruises around her throat.

I dropped the phone in horror and shuddered. Obviously, someone in Lutsen had been killed and Jake was investigating the murder. Probably taking pictures as evidence.

But wasn't he a Narcotics Officer?

I brushed it aside. It probably didn't mean anything when you were one of the first detectives at a crime scene. Still, it seemed like quite a coincidence – that we were vacationing at the same time a woman was murdered, and that Jake was around to help. The real question was, why would he send a gruesome picture like that to this other phone he had?

I picked up the phone once again, opened it back up, and went directly to the stored photos.

There were many.

As I began looking through the pictures, my blood ran cold. Most of them appeared to be of dead women. When I glanced at one in particular, I couldn't breathe.

"Darcy?" I whispered in horror, staring at her lifeless eyes under the bathwater. As I went back even further in the stored pictures, I noticed there was one taken of her sitting in the tub, very much alive, her face a mask of terror.

"No…" I moaned, dropping the phone.

Not Jake…please, God, don't let it be so!

Sobbing, I rushed to put on my jacket and boots, needing to get out of the cabin before he returned. There was no way I wanted to confront him with this. It didn't take a rocket scientist to understand the implication of those photos, especially the one of Darcy right before her death.

I grabbed the truck keys, my purse and threw open the front door.

"Whoa," smiled Jake, standing on the other side. "I'm here. No need to send out the troops."

I took a step backwards and stared at him in alarm.

He sighed. "I'm sorry. I know how worried you must have been. I went skiing and lost track of the time."

I opened my mouth to speak but nothing came out.

"Excuse me, babe," he said, brushing past me, carrying his skis.

"I was just going out," I said, hoarsely. "To get something to eat."

He set his equipment down and began pulling off his boots. "No need for that. There's food in the fridge. I'll make you something."

"Um, that's okay. I have a craving for some ice cream," I said. "We didn't bring any."

He walked over to me and put his hands on my shoulders. "We need to talk. Actually, *I* need to apologize. I was a total ass earlier. I know there isn't an excuse but please, let me make it up to you."

He stared at me with love in his eyes and my own filled up with bitter tears. How could someone so handsome and loving be so psychotic? "It's okay," I squeaked. "Really."

"No, it's not okay. I shouldn't have said those things to you; they were horrible and totally unacceptable. I hope you'll forgive me."

"It's fine."

He sighed. "There's something I have to tell you," he said. "I know I should have told you before, but I didn't want to scare you away."

I looked past him at his other phone, which was lying on the carpet. I knew I had to get the hell out of there before he noticed it. I forced a smile. "You know, it's okay. Really, whatever it is."

He shook his head. "No. It's not okay. In fact," he said, removing his jacket. "It's part of who I am and that's why you should know."

"I…"

He touched his stomach. "You know this scar on my abdomen?"

"Yes."

"Well, it was given to me by my father."

My eyes widened. "I thought you didn't know your father."

"Well, okay, my stepfather. He used to beat the shit out of me when I was a kid."

"Oh."

He nodded. "That's why I'm terrified of having kids. I don't know if I'd be any good at it and I don't have a lot of patience as it is. I'd never forgive myself if I raised my hand or lost my temper."

"But if you realize its wrong, you don't have to turn out like your parents." I looked into his eyes. "And if you have certain urges, ones that aren't normal, you should seek counseling, Jake."

He smiled. "I know. You're right. That's why I'm going to do everything it takes to be a damn good father. The truth is I'm excited about our baby, Lindsey. I was frightened at first, but now I can't wait. I just really want you to know that."

Obviously, killing the woman on the slopes had put him in better spirits. "That's great, Jake. I'm glad you're happy. Now, I really am craving ice cream, you know? So, I'll be back shortly."

He pulled me into his arms and planted a kiss on my lips. "Nonsense. You stay here and relax, babe. I'll get you some ice cream. What kind are you craving? Chocolate Chip, Rocky Road? Just tell me and I'll get it for you, my beautiful pregnant wife."

"Ah, just surprise me."

He released me and turned around to grab his jacket. "Okay."

"Thanks."

"Hey, where did this come from?" he asked, moving towards the flip-phone. He picked it up and a look of horror spread across his face.

Frightened, I turned and raced out of the cabin, towards the SUV. I unlocked the doors and jumped inside, placing the key in the ignition.

"Lindsey!" hollered Jake, rushing towards me in the darkness. "What are you doing?"

Trembling, I turned the key but heard only a "clicking" noise.

"Oh, my God!" I shrieked as my eyes met Jake's and he began to pound on the window.

"Lindsey, open up!"

Sobbing, I tried the engine again but still nothing happened.

He put his hand on the window and stared at me. "What's going on? Why are you doing this?"

"Leave me alone!" I cried, reaching in my purse for my cell phone, only to discover it was missing.

"Come on, Lindsey!"

Just when I thought all hope was lost, police lights flashed on the other side of the SUV. I breathed a sigh of relief; someone in one of the other cabins must have called the cops.

"Raise your hands and step away from the vehicle!" demanded the officer, as he got out of the squad car, gun raised.

Jake lifted his hands in the air and began backing away. Before he was able to take his third step, however, I heard the cop's gun go off and Jake dropped to the ground.

"You can come out of the vehicle, ma'am!" yelled the officer. "It's safe."

Shaking, I unlocked the door and got out. "Oh, my God," I shuddered, stepping over Jake's body. Part of me wanted to hold him in my arms, the other was horrified that I'd married such a cold-blooded killer.

"He won't be bothering anyone anymore," smiled the officer, staring down in satisfaction at Jake's body.

I stared at the cop and then gasped in horror when I recognized him. "Jerry?"

"That's right. Happy to see me?" he chuckled; now pointing the gun directly at me. "I'm happy to see you. I couldn't believe my luck when I found out that you were getting married."

"How…?"

"Patience, and friends in high places. Just because I moved doesn't mean I forgot how you murdered my brother, bitch."

"Please," I begged. "Don't hurt me."

"I'm not going to hurt you," he said, cocking the gun. "I'm going to kill you, so you actually feel nothing at all," he smiled coldly. "You know the old saying: revenge is sweet."

I glanced towards the other small cabins, hoping that someone would come to my rescue, but the rooms were all dark.

"Nobody's going to help you," he laughed. "Most of those other cabins are vacant at the moment. Must be the slower time of the year."

"Please," I begged in tears. "I'll do anything you want."

He moved towards me and grabbed my arm. "You know," he said. "I think I'll take my time killing you. It'll be much more fun."

"No, please, Jerry…"

Ignoring my protests, he pulled me towards the cabin and pushed me inside. Then, he pulled out a set of handcuffs, dragged me into the kitchen, and cuffed me to the metal refrigerator door handle.

"I'll be right back," he said. "Got to take care of that fucker's body before we get down to business."

I stared in terror as he left me and went back outside. Knowing I didn't have much time, I tried breaking the door handle, but it wouldn't even budge.

"Dammit!" growled Jerry, storming back into the cabin, seconds later. "I don't know how he did it, but I'll blow his fucking brains out when I find him."

"What's happening?" I asked.

Jerry glared at me. "He's somehow escaped."

As we stared at each other, the lights went out and Jerry began to really freak out. "Goddammit!" he raged. "Thinks he's smart, does he? Well, I got what he wants, so I'm running this fucking show! Come on, bitch," he spat, moving towards me. "We're getting the fuck out of here."

Once my hands were free, he grabbed my wrist and yanked me towards the door. "Don't you dare fuck with me, cunt," he warned. "Or I'll put a bullet in your head."

I bit my tongue as he pulled me into the darkness, his gun drawn.

"You'd better give yourself up, Sharp!" hollered Jerry. "Or I'll paint the snow with her blood! Make me one great fucking picture, too!"

A noise from somewhere behind the cabin startled us both. Jerry tightened his grip on my wrist and began pulling me in that direction. "Well, I know one thing for sure, that fucker is hurt," he said, motioning towards the speckles of blood on the snow. "He can't be too far."

I heard a creaking sound from somewhere above. We both turned as Jake fell from the top of an old shed sitting next to the cabin, landing on Jerry. I leaped away and watched as they rolled around in the snow together, wrestling for the gun.

I didn't hesitate.

I turned and rushed towards the front of the cabin, plowing through the snow in my heavy boots. When I heard the echo of the gunshots, I began to sob. Deep down, I knew I probably wasn't going to escape, not this time.

"Lindsey!" hollered Jake.

I turned and saw him limping towards me with the gun in his hand. I pushed myself faster.

"For the love of God, woman, stop running! I've been shot!"

Images of the dead women on his phone, especially the ones of Darcy, rushed through my mind. I ignored Jake and pushed myself faster. Unfortunately, what did me in was the clear ice on the driveway. As I moved, I miscalculated how slippery the black ice was, and landed flat on my back.

"Lindsey!" cried Jake, crouching down next to me.

I shoved him. "Don't touch me!"

"Wait," he said, trying to help me as I struggled to get up.

The sharp pains in my lower back were excruciating. "Please," I choked. "Just leave me alone."

He motioned behind him. "Lindsey, he's dead, honey. He can't hurt you."

"But you can," I cried as he grabbed my arm again. "Please let me go!"

He stared at me, incredulously. "Babe, I would *never* hurt you. *Never*!"

It was then that I felt the wetness between my legs and began to sob. I knew exactly what it meant.

"Oh, my God," he whispered in horror, seeing the blood on my pants. "Lindsey…"

"Call an ambulance," I moaned, turning my head away from his face. "Please."

Chapter Thirty-two

I stepped quietly into Jake's hospital room and moved towards the bed. His eyes were closed and he appeared to be sleeping. I pulled a chair out from the side of the room and moved it next to him.

His eyes opened. "Hey," he whispered, hoarsely.

I leaned forward and slid my hand over his. "Hey."

"I'm so sorry," he said, glancing at my stomach.

"No. It's not your fault. If anything, it was mine."

He frowned. "Why, because you thought I was some cold-blooded killer and was only trying to escape? Hell, if I found what you did, I'd think the same damn thing. Don't go blaming yourself, Lindsey."

I stared at Jake, still feeling guilty about accusing him of murder. When they'd found both of our cell phones in Jerry's possession, along with the murdered girl's body in the trunk of his squad car, I'd never been so relieved in my life. Apparently, the flip-phone containing the pictures of the dead women *had* been Jake's, the one that had been stolen over a year ago. Jerry had used it to take pictures of his and Parker's victims, starting with Darcy.

"I still can't believe that bastard found us, especially on our honeymoon," said Jake.

"He was a crafty son-of-a-bitch," I said. "In fact, I hadn't even realized our phones were missing. He must have broken into the cabin when we were skiing, took ours, and planted the other one."

He nodded. "He wanted to frame me, obviously, or at least, scare the hell out of you."

I laughed bitterly. "Well, he did a good job. I'm just glad he's not around anymore, plotting more revenge. He's already taken so much from me."

Jake sighed and slipped his fingers between mine. "You know, we can try again. In fact," he said, scooting over on the mattress. "Hop on up and we'll get started, right now."

I chuckled. "Right, you just survived a near-fatal shot in your side. Just get some rest, Detective. We have plenty of time to try again."

His face became serious. "Are you sure that *you're* okay?"

I stared at him for a minute and nodded. "Considering that I'm alive and still with the man I love, I'm doing just fine. The fact that we lost this child isn't easy, but I'm not going to let it tear me up inside."

"You're a strong woman and a wonderful mother. We're going to try again, Linds. I really want you to have our baby."

I smiled at all the emotions reflected in his eyes. "We'll talk about it later."

He kissed my knuckles. "Just remember, I love you, Mrs. Sharp."

"And I love you, Detective."

***

The End

Printed in Great Britain
by Amazon